Breathing Underwater

D1131646

by the same author
PIG TALES
MY PHANTOM HUSBAND

Breathing Underwater

MARIE DARRIEUSSECQ

translated by
Linda Coverdale

faber and faber

First published in France as *Le Mal de Mer* in 1999
by P. O. L. éditeur
First published in Great Britain in 2001
by Faber and Faber Limited
3 Queen Square London WC1N 3AU

Photoset by Agnesi Text, Hadleigh, Suffolk
Printed in England by Clays Ltd, St Ives plc

A CIP record for this book
is available from the British Library

ISBN 0–571–20328–0

2 4 6 8 10 9 7 5 3 1

I live by the ocean
and during the night
I dive into it
down to the bottom
underneath all currents
and drop my anchor

this is where I'm staying
this is my home

Björk Gudmundsdóttir

This book is dedicated to the memory of Melsene Timsit.

1

It's a mouth, half open, breathing, but the eyes, nose, and chin are no longer there. It's a mouth bigger than any mouth imaginable, rending space in two, expanding it, so that you have to swivel your body in a semicircle to try seeing it all. The noise – the breathing – is tremendous, but above all it's that you don't expect it: you climb up the dune, you struggle to drag your feet up the slope, for a while all you're concerned with is this suction beneath the sand, and suddenly space explodes, you've looked up and the top of the dune has fallen away far below you, something like two colossal arms opening wide – but that's not it exactly, it's not welcoming, it's rather that you have no choice, the way you'd fall off a building or a monument without a guardrail. It's hard to visualize the edge of this thing, hard to decide precisely where it is, how far away. Before, you were climbing the dune, already hearing the noise but not yet feeling anything on your face, leaning into the sand, in the cold dry smell of the sand, and then the noise grows, seeming to spread out even behind your head, a 360-degree noise, although the sea is straight ahead, blowing in your face, evaporating the sweatiness of the uphill climb with a raspy breath, salty but not humid, dried by the still-scorching expanse of the beach.

She goes over the climb in her thoughts, to recover that moment (even though the sea is there in front of her and fills her whole head), to relive that moment when space split asunder, sprang out to the sides, and liquefied into this black mass, thrusting back the edges of the sky and dissolving them, drinking them, breathing through millions of red slits opening and closing on the motionless black mass, through millions of little mouths on the enormous closed black mouth where a pale gleam lingers at the place where the sun flicked out its tongue. To rediscover that moment when, all of a sudden, the dune became the sea, you would have to go back down, start once more, close your eyes and pretend to have forgotten, opening them again only at the top, absorbing the shock without flinching, forcing your body to stand there facing the void. But the sun has set, the sky overhead has turned black and is slowly descending, folding the sea over on itself, and that's it for the first time; now she has seen the sea.

Her face is as if washed with it, opened up, and her

mother believes that – that you can tell from people's faces, especially children's, who has seen the şea and who has not: those who must have welcomed the sweep of the sea into their eyes (crashing all the way to the backs of their skulls, it empties them out, in a way), and those who were able only to dream it, from pictures or words, those who have tried, confusing the sea and infinity, to keep adding a little bit more to the image, telling themselves that even beyond, still further, without end, the sea goes on . . . when it's not that at all, when, compared to galaxies, the sea is minuscule. She passes her hand over the little girl's face, a round face, undefined, made even less defined by the impact of the sea: a broadening of the cheeks, the gaze, the fluttering of metamorphosis beneath the skin; a boundless childhood, distended, pelagic. They would have to stay there, right there in that moment, to let it last as long as that grandeur demands. She feels, rolling beneath her fingertips, the sand grains that microscopically graze the surface of this face, until the little girl shakes herself and blinks, perhaps to recover that first moment of the sea, or to get rid of the sand and of course, impatiently, the hand.

She leaves the child on top of the dune. She feels something like relief, a pause; the intuition that she can leave her there, absorbed by the sea, eyes straining from their sockets; in the redundancy of the fishing poles, sinkers, floats, and even the buckets and shovels. She won't rush down to the beach straight away, she won't run off to drown in the waves; unlike logs blazing in fireplaces or outdoor bonfires, the sea does not make itself our friend, it doesn't crackle within arm's reach: you look at it a long time before it dawns on you that you can touch it. She opens the boot of the car. The tent is there, where they leave it from one holiday to the next; she takes out the sweaters, the blanket, the hard-boiled eggs in their Tupperware box, the torch. She's much calmer than she was on the motorway. She has this feeling now of having thought of everything. The torch works, illuminating heather at the foot of the trees, and craters of sand. The ten thousand francs are in her pocket; she must stop worrying that they'll fall out, that the wind will snatch them away, that the child will play with them. The wad of notes is already a little depleted; she was given coins as change when she bought the bread roll and the orange juice. Slowly, she retraces her steps; she has the eggs, the blanket, they're all set, that's what they're going to do: eat and sleep here. The little girl is a slight bump on the crest of the dune, a hummock haloed in dark purple. Too recently raked by the sun for stars to be peeping through so soon, the sky behind her is like tar, unless that's the ocean; she has climbed high enough to see it, she has passed that point where the noise seems to issue no longer – muffled – from the dune, but from all of nocturnal space. She would like the child to see it and, dreading a struggle, she wraps her in the blanket; she should see it, the way the horizon melts into the sea because eyes seared by the sunset can no longer tell sky from water, or because at the sun's zenith and at twilight there are, as with a tide on the turn, an inertia of light: one bright and the other dark, one diurnal, the other nocturnal, eroding in turn the heights or the horizon; so it is at this crepuscular hour, when the day-laden sea swells and cracks, and when fingers run through hair produce a humming and electric sound.

On one side she senses the presence of the trees, their black crests; on the other, this emptiness, also black, but flat, immense, into which her body leans, restrained at the neck by the scratchy blanket. Her mother holds her so close that her buttocks are lifted slightly off the sand. She's tired, and would like to go home and sleep. The red mouths have vanished. If she were to wriggle free, if she were to get up and run, she would realize, but too late, that one side of her is missing: her leg would suddenly slip or be dislocated or shrink, she would be teetering on a stump, unsupported, felled by this absence of ground or foot. The eggs become a dry paste on her tongue: the smooth white and the earthy yolk mix together as they stick to the roof of her mouth; the saliva won't flow quickly enough, it's as if egg – egg paste – is what her mouth is secreting now, a wax smeared over her gums and gullet. On the motorway, she swallowed the bread roll down with the orange juice, but apparently her mother didn't think to bring along any water. Asking her for some is a delicate proposition, that's if any sound could still penetrate the egg; she might start shouting, she's easily upset. The egg in the throat descends, stretching the gullet walls, requiring faster breathing and giving the impression it's going to get stuck at the point where the neck joins the thorax, beneath the fold emphasized by the blanket as though she were nothing but a doll with a cloth body, a stitched bag about to swallow but inside which the puppeteer's hand, as everyone knows, is moving to mimic the living organs. Her mother shakes her and she is hollow once more, resonant, famished; as she was on the motorway before the bread roll, in the car that seemed (once the joy of sitting in front with the seatbelt under her chin had worn off) so different, facing the windscreen full of that straight, unfamiliar road, which did not lead back home. In the glow of the torch, her mother, as she goes down the dune again, is long and black like the pines, a pine with arms and legs, from which emanate pale beams of light fanning out into the undergrowth.

She has forgotten the water; there isn't anything else in the car boot except the tent and the school satchel. She could so easily have asked her mother for some water when she picked up the child, but what reason could she have given – a Thermos, a bottle, for a trip supposedly of three suburban streets, lasting five minutes? Further on, she never thought to buy any: from the very first kilometres of sunshine, a migraine – exhausting and familiar – had taken up all the space, leaving no room for other feelings. That's it, it's got her again: in the left temple, throbbing beneath the bone; a single point, fixed, small, a pellet you could simply tear out, but its transmitting range encompasses her isolated and ringing skull. As on the radar screen of a submarine, its beam scanning for torpedoes, the pain glowing more fiercely with each heartbeat, her body reeling from the impact – her whole body and not simply her head: a staggering shock. She would have to leave herself completely behind, like a sloughed skin, as she is generating, like people exposed to atomic radiation, an aura that consumes her. She lowers the lid of the boot gently; it's not enough, you have to slam it. She feels her energy draining away. Up there, on the dune, the child doesn't seem to be looking anywhere in particular; all you can make out, against the nocturnal lustre of the sea, is a suggestion of her profile, slightly inclined, a medallion of indifference (and yet the sea for the first time, the surprise of bringing her to the shore, a five-hour drive away . . .). She picks up the tent and moves forward, her head enormous around the tiny central point of the migraine, her body snapping in pain like a sheet on a clothes line; what is scouring her out like this, hurtling around freely inside her, certainly cannot be contained within her body but must surely – how to put it – be audible, visible, at least perceivable, giving off light, and she's being tracked at a distance, as if she were lugging a transmitter; moreover the tent, the blanket, and the satchel are booby-trapped. She hesitates, and her feet slip on the steep sand. But no one could have anticipated, imagined, forewarned; no one can follow them.

She's not entirely sure that it is the sea. She would have liked some advance notice, to prepare herself; it's a bit like the day her mother took her to see a film for the first time, and she was frightened, even if she now enjoys going over in her head the moment when her mother parks in an unfamiliar spot, not very far from the house, but on a strange street, one that looks like the street the house is on but that opens, through a big door, on to a deep hole, with a flight of stairs, where a giant gullet grooved with red arches now gapes, making her scream in terror from the audience; now, though, she'd like to start over again, now that she knows, slipping once again into the darkness and even into the belly of the whale, laughing at the vertigo and then clinging to the raft with Pinocchio. She thought today, as she has often hoped, that they were going to see a film, she really believed and hoped so since the streets weren't exactly those leading home, because they were leaving grandmother's not by following the canal but by turning left, towards the main road, the one they go down, usually, on market days. But the city got bigger. From the car windscreen flowed new streets, at the end of which burst a sheaf of other streets, spreading out in other directions; the windscreen is crazed from all those streets turning, dividing, spreading out, framed for a moment in the wing and rearview mirrors and zig-zagging with pedestrians, then gliding smoothly, walls washed, edges erased, streets that divide and reopen, constantly shifting the depth of space until they gather together in a grey trench, long and straight, fluted with slits and roughened with rhythmic white. She's not entirely sure that it is the sea – perhaps she slept a while before arriving at these dunes; she's missing a stage, something between the grandmother, the streets, the motorway and the bread roll, and then the sea. She sat in the front seat, wondering about seeing a film and, what do you know, the proud streets were brought low, replaced by greens and yellows, leaning telephone poles, a flat, swiftly flowing landscape; then something soft oozes into the car, as though wafted in by the shimmering black roof, or the heat; she sinks slowly into the seat as the foam rubber beneath the fabric gradually gives way, swallowing her from behind, a deglutition, hesitant velvety lips that suck in, then half let go, following the cadence of the road. She opens the window all the way when her mother stops to fill the tank and the smell of petrol seeps into her stomach. A little further along is the shopping centre, where her mother takes so long to buy her a snack. The car park is almost empty. The air between the cars is warped. She slides across the seat, stretches her feet towards the pedals, tries turning the wheel. The mirages tremble. The store windows blow bubbles of sunlight. The shopping trolleys carve cubes from a kind of grey jelly that quivers between the metal bars, bounces off the asphalt. Forms slowly thicken, legs take shape where only grey ripples floated before, eyes and nostrils poke through faces. Cars drive off. She wants so much to cry she can hardly bear it. Her mother is huge all of a sudden, completely covering the windows. Then the windscreen fills with white sky as crash barriers rush by, rising and falling. Her mother is practically lying across her lap, acrobatically closing the window, driving with one hand; her hair is loose and seems somehow naked, brushing against her, light streaks bleached amid the darker mass. And now she's on this dune, her mouth plastered shut with egg. Shouldn't the sky be blue, the waves white, the horizon marine and sprinkled with sails? The sea, if it is the sea, appears to have poured down from the black sky, capsizing into a liquid night, the weighted base of a tumbling world that keeps the sky in balance. It laps gently; without that faint noise you wouldn't see it, you'd feel only that heaviness preventing you from pulling your feet out of the sand and running; that low-lying mass, that tremendous condensation of shadow, beneath a sky hissing with the wind that separates them.

Occasionally, there where a breeze suggests a line perhaps a touch greyer, a fold smoothed out immediately, large glimmering globules seem to surface, showing you where the sky is, blue globes that are soon engulfed again, leaving briefly behind only a dull fluorescence, no doubt from jellyfish; perhaps, tomorrow, without going too close to the water's edge, she'll be able to point them out to the child; she thinks she remembers that in daylight, jellyfish – that kind, at least – look like bowler hats, as if men were strolling around beneath them. That's what she needs: to float about, let the waves wash through her; the migraine would melt, dissolving in the flood; her brain would become a bluish globule, empty, aqueous and soft, bearing the weight of her body as though she were sleepwalking under the sea. In the meantime the tent must be set up; the stars have not come out, and it might rain.

She holds the tent pegs carefully, between her tightly closed hands. There are twelve of them: she hasn't lost a single one since last year. The tent is spread out on the sand for the moment, a big blue bag that flutters and assumes unexpected shapes. The year before, when all three of them went to the mountains, she was in charge of the pegs even then but the method seemed more reliable: her father inside with the tent poles, her mother outside with the guy ropes, the two of them shouting, but when the tent finally went up, revealing this hollow inside, within fabric panels that had been so flat before, the night became habitable. She slept sandwiched between them, her head at their necks and her feet by their knees, wedged between two tent poles; by stretching out her toes she could make the entire tent shimmy. The sheep's dreams were little tinkling bells. Through the blue folds, made even bluer by the darkness, you could make out the stars, bright haloes in the woven cloth, revealing the warp and weft as if through a magnifying glass. Fabric, bells, a mountain stream, the night: things were close, and the tent formed the membrane, within and without, between her own skin and the world, just thick enough to contain, among the smells of grass and mildew, the warmth of their breathing. The tent is heaving on the sand now, reminding her of the cat tied up in a bag and dropped from a balcony during a birthday party. The pegs won't hold firm in the sand; her father used a mallet for the hard mountain earth. Something under the trees wails like a saw, wings rustling. Then she sees the blue fabric above her head. Little bells still seem to be ringing in her ears, but the stars aren't shining through, as if the cloth were sheathed by a second roof, black and opaque, which has to be thought of (when it trembles, whipped by the wind, in rapid stripes) as suspended from the shadow of the pines. The sand hums, from rhythmic pounding. She isn't touching anything, she isn't moving, the ground is level, but she keeps rolling over. And now her feet are sticking out beyond the tent poles.

She has the ten thousand francs, in her pocket; she touches the wad of notes and the few coins. She didn't feel up to getting undressed, or to making the child do so, either. They haven't brushed their teeth; anyway, there isn't any water. After all, perhaps it will be cold tonight, and she'll be happy the child is sleeping in her clothes, as the blanket is thin. She could have bought a sleeping bag and some extra sweaters this afternoon, but didn't think of it. That's because of the migraine. Next to the petrol station she saw first the green-cross sign outside the pharmacy, then the white overall, behind a counter. It's a nuisance having to get out the whole wad of notes; it looks strange, obviously. The paracetamol, taken immediately, seems to take the edge off the pain. She can still see the car quite clearly, and the child as well: hands gripping the steering wheel, she's probably making engine noises. After buying the snack, she'll still have about 9,950 francs left. It's a big supermarket, with automatic doors; when she walks into the gaze of the little red eye, gusts of cold air bathe her in an icy breath. Leave the child, go out the other side, someone will find her, of course they will, and as for her – ten thousand francs, a plane ticket. She walks through the red eye, wearing just that light sundress; the little wheels squeak, the entrance gate is there, hip high, two automatic barriers painted with white arrows; the biscuit and fizzy-drink shelves are probably far away at the other end. Light falls downwards into the supermarket, a light that has passed through windows, yellow and exhausted, with blotches that must be leaves or insects made gigantic by their shadows. People push past her; each time the barriers open, the arrows point to the invisible back of the store, then close again to indicate the tiny target at their junction, a point one centimetre wide; she turns away and finds herself facing some small shops. The Danish pastries have a greasy sheen; she asks for a bread roll and an orange juice; against her belly she feels the burning hot roll and the chilled can, although she would have preferred a bottle for the child. Now night has fallen and is creaking everywhere. The roof of the tent sags: she managed to drive in the pegs but couldn't pull the guy ropes tight enough. She might have thought for a moment, one moment, about what they needed, even if it was only water. That limp blue material above her face, almost touching it – she could cry.

In school this morning no one was talking about holidays yet. The teacher had just handed out permission slips for the end-of-the-year trip, she wants the signatures of both parents. She put them in her school satchel, but now that she thinks about it – did they bring it with them, from grandmother's? She stretches and wiggles her toes, discreetly, knees drawn up to her stomach; the ground is hard, compacted. If she moves, she feels grains of sand slipping away beneath the plastic, out from under her, a silent fall, and then a lump, a ridge, cement that solidifies and bruises. Her back is itching; insects, maybe, scrambling around, struggling beneath her weight, tunnelling, scratching their carapaces on the grains of sand. She'd have to go outside, very quietly, find the car keys, and rummage around for the satchel. A tingling climbs her cheek; her muscles tighten like rubber bands. Her mother seems to be sleeping. Spiders, *Coleoptera*, stag beetles, and earwigs are everywhere; the sand is so fluid you need only dig between two roots, let the warm grains shower down on you, and mingle your six or eight legs with the six or eight legs of your nest mates, in order to doze off lazily, conscious only – sweetly, erratically – that all the wing sheaths have begun to stir, without your knowing any more whether it's you or one of your neighbours whirring like that, fast asleep.

The night is purple through the blue fabric, the moon must have risen; now only the branches – or, rather, the spliced crests of the pines – weave black cables around the tent, and something mauve hoots along with the rasping of the crickets: an owl, a night bird; she turns her head slowly towards the child, her eyelids are squeezed shut, her small fists rubbing against her cheeks. She appears to be asleep. She picks up one of her wrists, so slender, and unfolds the fingers with her own; the silly thing is still biting her nails. The owl has stopped screeching and the crickets singing. She can't get to sleep; not that she was really counting on sleep-ing, but she would have liked at least to have a bit of a break from the migraine. Things are creeping beneath the tent; inexplicably, they stop moving, buried in the ground, imperceptible when still. The wind slips through the trees, almost silently, skimming the dune, skimming the tent, as if the world were as sleek as pine needles. The mass of sand doesn't give beneath her back, pulls her down and holds her, limbs, chest, neck, head. The sound of the sea grows louder, filling in those holes in space where both birds and insects have gone quiet. Yet what she hears is like an exaggeration of the silence, a liquid, material silence, underlying the tick-tock of the blood in her skull and the irregular jolts of a branch swishing, bark peeling away, the crunch of a pile of pine needles; the ultra-soft whisper of the sand, per-haps, beneath the step of a prowler. She listens, and the silence grows even more vast, filling the tent to the very brim, throbbing at her ear-drums. The steps draw closer and she holds her breath – it's a respiration that glides over the sand, in waves: she loses it if she listens for it (then the migraine pounds louder), and finds it again with the sea, the rustling, the sudden crescendos, so that sometimes, instead of this one distinct footfall, it seems that the dune and the forest are on the move. She opens the zip; the night pours in, vast and violet, streaked by the pines. The air is cool, the sand grows cold beneath her feet. No one can find them.

She called her several times, *Mum–my*: she watches her move along the crest of the dune, the black shape of the dress opening and closing on the sandy slope; she's going to go down the other side. The tent opening is flapping, scraping the zip against a pole; the fabric slithers, puffs up, collapses. The pines stand still, on the alert. Someone's going to come, with a knife, big boots that will leave deep puddles of blood, and all they'll find will be thick black crusts; there, over by the bristling undergrowth, something is moving that is neither holly nor heather: a spine, fur, eyes, a quadruple row of teeth and claws. Did her mother leave the torch? You can hear a belly scooting over the scrubby gorse; it must be a lizard, or a tiny mouse; a hedgehog, a porcupine, an armadillo, an anteater, a tiger. In South America there are bats as big as people, they look like sacks of potatoes hanging upside down among the leaves; they wait for travellers to fall asleep then, after they've dozed off under the trees, the bats cover them with their large wings, and bend down; beneath these warm membranes, which hide the moon, the traveller senses only the depths of sleep and night into which he lets himself sink, as his blood drains from him. She buries her head in the folds of the tent and the universe turns back into a big blue skirt stretched a little out of shape.

She takes off her shoes, shakes them, pours out the glistening grains. The humidity has made the sand stick together; her nails scratch out clumps, cubes. The night is black and gashed with foam. The waves fall from high in the sky and the moon tumbles in silvery glints that shear, crackling, through the shadows. Holding your hand straight out in front, you could just touch them with your fingertips. She takes a step back; lighthouses are screwed into the hinges of the sky. The sea is a vertical partition through which you need only to pass: water would slide from nose to cheeks, from chest to back, from belly to hips to buttocks – and flow together again; entering the sea would be like going through curtains. The sand gives way, deeply, with every step, ringing her ankles in a chill dampness; she will walk to the lighthouse, then on to the next one; when day comes she'll go to a café and sit outside, and in the evening she'll get a room with a view.

She can see the satchel on the back shelf in the car; her mother must have moved it. The phone card and her home number are underneath the flap, in case she ever gets lost. But this forest is larger, it seems, than all the forests she knows; they drove through it for a long time. She saw her face in the passenger wing mirror (one eye, half a nose, and a close-up of her hand), and behind it that constant, fleeting, patchwork impression of the forest: black and white flashes, streaming from the car as if from a lamp held high, cleaving space in long empty slices that banged against the windows, a thrumming of air. It has all faded; a nocturnal dishevelment grips the creaking, abandoned trees. Something sleeps in the forest, walks there, somnambulistic and as tall as the tree trunks. She climbs the dune; the sand yields to the fresh footfalls. Now the tent is very small, almost invisible, blue on blue. The trunks crouch in the darkness. She's on an island; if she calls out, everything will awaken. A long white fold creases the sky. She feels herself slowly slewing round; set down on the dune and beneath the sky. The sea has invaded everywhere: black water has flowed into insect nests, craters in the sand, the furrows of roots, has drunk up footprints and forest, flooding the night. The air withdraws whenever the sea inhales, then returns, before the water swells again, taking up all the space, so that one cannot breathe except in small gulps, between two immense movements of the sea, between two tremors of the sky: by hiccuping, with streaming cheeks, and the oyster taste of seaweed on the tongue.

2

She was exactly the same as always; she kissed the child, asked if everything had gone well. Everything had: she talked about school, coming back from school, having something to eat, the nature programme at five-thirty, homework. She was a bit late, as she was on evenings when she had something to do first. Her hair was loose, which made her look young, almost childlike, and then there was the sundress – had she worn it to work? A blue sundress, with straps crossed at the back. Perhaps it's the heat: you slip on a dress, one you wouldn't wear, normally, in town, and it gives you ideas. Maybe they've gone to see a film. Or they're at a swimming pool open late at night, with fountains, slides, refreshing spray. Opening the windows doesn't help – there's not a breath of air. She could have left a note, it's true. At one point, while the child was collecting her things (she didn't seem in a hurry, she was almost relaxed, letting the little girl take her own sweet time), she ran some water in the kitchen, you could hear it in the living room; when she went in five minutes later she was still there, leaning with both hands on the edge of the sink, bending over slightly, and the thought occurred to her: thin, too thin, the straps crossed over the sinuous spine as fragile as moss stitch knitted under the skin. Because it was one of those moments when, even if you reach out, you don't think you can touch the hologram standing in front of you (but pass through its listless body, perhaps, disturbing its ghost with your fingers): she saw her there, deaf, blind, vulnerable, so sure she was alone that her body had gone limp, bearing down heavily on her wrists, shoulders hunched, her weight over one hip, backbone bent, ankles flexed to one side over high-heeled strap-sandals, swaybacked, hanging suspended there, a grown-up, a stranger. She looks at the back, the crossed straps – it takes a second, the time to see her: the length of the bones, the buckled ankles, dark roots under the bleached hair; she reaches out, automatically, to turn the tap off; the back shivers, the collarbones drop, the shoulder blades come together; the face turns, irritated in advance. She asks if the child is ready. Her cheeks are covered with a mist of droplets (she probably rinsed her face in her cupped hands) and a few tendrils of hair are sticking to her neck. As for her, she talks about the heat. About how the child was bathed in perspiration when she got out of school, about how there isn't adequate ventilation. But they've already gone. She stays there, in the empty flat, in the light-and-shade stripes of the shutters. The net curtains barely stir, an illusion, a longing for coolness – unless a breeze sneaked into the apartment when they left and the after-noon is at last relaxing its grip. The shutters cast soft-ened beams into the dim light, dust is suspended in the air, luminous and oblique; if she stretches out her hand, or simply breathes a little deeply, she sees the fine motes, rubbed smooth against the furniture by the passing hours, begin to tremble; she feels – fleetingly – a draught return, doors opening, the square of light and the two shadows across the threshold. In southern Japan, in the humid heat of the summer, delicate bells are hung in the windows; fans dangle from their bamboo, basalt, tin, or porcelain clappers: at the slightest breath, the pleated paper sweeps the bell along in a subtle song that eases the air. She crosses the living room, picks up the cups, a pencil left by the child; the curtains hang stiffly, a gauze sculpture. But if she stares at them, or if she looks just to the side, at the wall, as if catching them unawares, she sees them sway, out of the corner of her eye: the fine check pattern deepens, one window becomes two, white reflections flutter loose in folds, in

curves, and the forms appear, shoulders raised, hips tilt-
ed, quivering gently with repressed energy. That's
something she cannot tell her son-in-law: that she saw
her, that she saw them, in the curtains, and in the door-
way; that she often sees them, just after they've left, and
occasionally at night. Of course it's the dust, iridescent in
the sun between the shafts of shadow, weaving fingers,
hair, hips. He's in front of her, she's not sure he's listen-
ing, he takes his head in his hands. He has already done
everything he had to, the hospitals, the police, and now
he's talking about consulting a private detective. It's still
too soon, however; they might be seeing a film, the last
show. It's a night that feels like the onset of summer.
The heat has lifted, a little. She was the same as always,
just exactly the same. She was staring at something in
the sink. Her body was tense, crumpled, compact,
crisply outlined against the light, yet at the same time
suspended, from the collarbones, you might say, so that
another body, more fluid, came loose and leaned forward, but shielded from the light, volatile and fluctuat-
ing, blurred, in front of the opaque body, connected to it
only at the shoulders, by the crossed straps.

Can you think of anyone? Anyone she might have gone
to? Eighty per cent of the time, people consult him

about adultery. Here, there's the kid, to complicate matters. He sees a few cases of missing persons, a new life, a sea-change, through the looking-glass: men, always; in debt, homicidal, in love, or worn out. You can't make them come back; you can make them pay up, sometimes. She'll do what they do. She'll make a mistake. Maybe she has already used a phone card or a credit card. He takes the photos. He puts them in his pocket with the cheque. The two men shake hands.

The people here speak Spanish. They noticed it when they bought fruit and water. The border isn't much more than a loop in the road and a blue flag with stars on it. When she reversed, the child woke up. The sharp bend of the slip road, the motorway again, going up and down hills, winding; purple mountains and fields full of darkness, trees with broad green leaves.

She'd been asleep until now. The sun beats against the window. She sees herself in the rearview mirror: creased eyelids, tousled hair, red nose, light shining through translucent nostrils and all the way in if she tips her head back. The air is already quite hot. Grains of sand are shifting about under her T-shirt and scratching her; ants, maybe. Her mother has stopped again. Her new dress is creased where she's been sitting. Perhaps she bought it yesterday, just before she came to pick her up. She comes back smelling of vanilla and hair spray; the old woman she was speaking to is still pointing the way. The landscape passes across all the glass, the left window, the windscreen, the right window: a river, the shade beneath the trees, lines of houses, and perhaps, beyond, if one went on long enough, without any more changes of direction, straight ahead, no stopping – the house, the market, the cinema. Something of the grandmother now hovers in the car, with the hair spray and the vanilla, the way it does in the shuttered flat when she goes there after school. Only because of the scratchy sand can she believe that she really spent the night on the dunes, overlooking the sea and the woods – or, rather, that this dream is one of the ones that, when the sleeper awakes, leaves behind (next to the bed, by the door, on the skin) a sign, a tattoo, a trace: the letter received in the nightmare, lying folded in four on the bedside table; the visitor's footprints; the broken pane of glass, where a scrap of his cape, a claw, a tuft of fur is snagged; and perhaps, after the dream of the sea, the salty hair at daybreak, the anklets of seaweed. She'd like to have a bath. She's cold, in spite of the sun. In South America, explorers who have fallen asleep in the arms of vampire bats never lose the two tiny red dots on their necks: all their lives, no matter how much they rub, they'll carry the mark of their journey through the forests, and every evening, behind their eyelids, they'll see once more the bloodless wings bending tenderly over their faces, solicitously enclosing the darkness. They'll be afraid to fall asleep.

The worst thing is thinking about the child during the night: was she cold, was she scared? Light and dark mingle, entwine, collapse and rise again, like a flowing river, a road streaming by. When her son-in-law telephoned, early that morning, to say they still hadn't come home, she'd said nothing; she'd slipped on her dressing-gown and closed both sets of curtains, making the room darker, setting the walls and furniture turning, slowly. She should have kept them there, said something. With her son-in-law, yesterday, and this morning on the phone – wanting him to be quiet or go away, since he would believe nothing of what she might say, since he would see nothing of the curtains moving, the water trickling from the tap, the shoulders beneath their straps, the shadows saturated with pollen. And he might accuse her of helping them run away. Outside cars brake or drive off; she hears children on the way to school. A ray of light darts between the velvet curtains, setting the airborne tinder aflame. She feels the blood in her hand, in her wrist, in her arm up to her shoulder, she feels the arteries and veins, the red heat overflowing her lungs and then draining away little by little; her heart beats too quickly, and a pain eats into her chest. The curtains flap, there's a flash of light that vanishes, the glare throbs, swells, then ebbs, leaving sparks in the eyes and a tingling in the fingers. Her cheeks and eyes burn; drifting glassy spheres drag long bright tails behind them, they dive too deep, she's in the dark, she rises again, searching for air, a flash shatters the surface, fine white lines, far away, something that's now as big as the sky and that stops, there. She raises the curtain; the street is awash with daylight. There's a tree that breaks the heart, a reminder that other trees exist and that simply strolling beneath their foliage would allow you to breathe again, to drink, tipping your head back, looking up at their clear and rippling water.

Sand has impacted in the toes of her trainers: hard, gritty balls between her toes, that work patiently, meticulously, prising off the nails. Hairy little tendrils have latched on to the laces, along with seeds, bits of insects, burs. Her mother blinks in the sunshine, studying the shop signs as they walk along the seafront. She waits for her on a bench, kicks off her trainers. She'd like to have the same footwear as the children here. There's an exotic contrast between their backpacks (surfers' backpacks, fluorescent with rainbow flaps) and their plastic sandals, soft as jelly. Her mother goes into some shops; the crossed straps of her sundress make two distinct dark lines behind the reflections in a shop window, behind the children chasing one another, in the opaque whiteness of the sun. Birds fly by in the window, black, pointed, flapping like batting eyelashes. If she changes position slightly, she can see houses by swimming pools, palm trees, beaches, smiling families holding hands, a small boy on his father's shoulders, a dog sitting on his haunches: photos stuck under the glass. Right next to the bench is a phonebox. The satchel was left in the car, a long way off, in another part of town. The dress in the window sways gently; the window is glossy with sunlight. Shifting her line of sight, she watches this jutting angle become a hollow; that black shadow, a double white profile; this armchair, a crouching beast; that recess, an exit to the jetty. A shimmering blue is revealed, as if in a false-bottomed boat. She can imagine she's inside a big house, sitting in front of bay windows overlooking the sea: a blue that's very pale, at first, then a dark line, and then more blue, darker, furrowed with white, grey, green, then a large patch of turquoise growing ever larger.

Birds are chirping: martins; the window is full of swooping martins, gliding motionless the instant after a wing beat. They pepper the sun with little eclipses. You'd think there was some brass mechanism, springs to magnify the birds at the edge of the bottle glass of the window, then grab them in midair and gather them together in miniature. All that's missing is the snow, to shake up in a plastic globe, a memento of a blue place where martins fly. She lets the curtain fall back. The voices of the children outside, the noise of them chasing each other over the cobbles, breaks into her brain, straining her skull at the joins. Her chest still hurts; she goes to lie down and wait.

A simple wrist movement, the steering wheel turning this way instead of that, the changing landscape, the kid silent with surprise, uneasiness, and the scenery persisting stubbornly and marvellously (or even: without you realizing it) in its strangeness – he understands all that, and the kind of emptiness of those alterations, which one must drive past, reject, going further, until one finds something truly empty, completely new. The client won't believe you can't find everything (proof of purchase, hotel bookings, road-toll receipts), eavesdrop on their conversations via satellite, track their heartbeats.

He spends the morning and the evening at the office. He plans to have their pictures appearing in the press, distributed at railway stations, in motorway service areas. He's amazed by how porous borders can be, by the indifference of space, of roads, by their continuity, by the breadth of continents, by the vastness of the sea. As for the client, he listens to him, it's part of the job. He tries to contain the reflexes of anguish: posters, the purchase of a weapon, the occupation of a police station, a hunger strike. As for the rest, one must be patient.

She hasn't used her credit card yet. She's paying for everything in cash, having emptied the joint account before leaving, ten thousand francs. Soon she'll be forced to find something else. If she hasn't left the country, she might feel she should enrol the kid in school, but it's coming up to the end of May, and even supposing she tries this, they might make her wait until September. He makes himself some coffee, looks at the photos again. Putting himself in her place, behind her eyes, behind her forehead; lifting her hair, seizing the thoughts beneath the smooth surface; seeing the roads, the trees, the places, the people. He would go and see her, show her his card; he'd tell her they've been looking for her, and how many days the investigation has been going on. She'd open her eyes wide, brush back her hair. It would be sunny, as in the photograph, and he would have to lean across, move forward to look at her. The lens has cast a bright reflection on her face, three circles of decreasing size, edged with white around a rainbow centre, three circles that – if you stop to consider them – are stars blurred by their own light. One of these circles rests on an eye, blotting out the iris, and if you really look, if for a moment you could block the brain's automatic compensation, creating the unseen detail of a woman's face (routinely filling in the eyes, nose, mouth, and the appropriate shape), then the face you would see is almost one-eyed, a blind spot on the iris of the right eye, the left strangely displaced by a lock of hair whose movement, at this angle, has been flattened against the middle of her forehead; and that sun-splash, scoring the eyelid but crossing the nose as well, with a last round flash falling at the corner of the lips, curtailing the smile, so that the mouth has been left lopsided, unfinished.

Great chunks of cliff lie on the beach, lined up in the order of their collapse; grass and trees still grow on them, pieces of the gardens above, diced into cubes and showing, in geological cross-section, the thin layer of green lawn, then the tangle of roots, then sandy clay –

ochre, wormholed by rivulets of water – and a final layer of grit, the whole snapped off as cleanly as a broken piece of pottery. Askew, a tamarisk shades the waves; the soil has crumbled away from roots as big as branches, stretching forlornly towards the salt water, writhing in botanic agony. She looks up; there remains, where the cliff has sheared off, a hollow indentation, a negative of what has fallen, the outline of a cavity that is mottled and smooth, as if the earth had undertaken not to slip any more; and just above, the ruins of some rotunda, greenhouse, orangery, or winter garden (people were dancing, drinking – painters, aviators, crooks with pigskin luggage, White Russians, their noses stuffed with cocaine), a section of colonnade, part of a leaded-glass window, shattered tiles, and then foundations encasing blocks of air, gutted basements, cellars plunging into pits, and deeper still, towards the beach, long, naked metal rods, the roots of reinforced concrete. If a body had been concealed there, it would have tumbled down with the cliff, mummified, sitting exposed in the shadow of the ghostly tamarisk. The child is looking somewhere else, nowhere in particular, perhaps where the town meets the sea, towards the mountains growing hazy with heat. She really should buy her an ice-cream.

The sea has emptied one entire side of the landscape.

To the left there are red and white houses, deserted cafés, an ice-cream seller, and then the pale curve of the mountains; to the right, as if the earth had sunk for lack of beach, there is only the sea, absent, blue, motionless under a radiant glaze. The children in plastic sandals have disappeared; a few old ladies stroll idly along, preceded by rigidly taut leads and little dogs straining forward, their forepaws in the air and their noses blue with asphyxia. She'd like to turn back now. With each step her trainers methodically chafe the soles of her feet. They're heading towards the ice-cream man. Heart pounding, she strains to read the labels on the coloured tubs. Her heels are burning. The hand holding hers is squeezing harder. She must choose; she can have two scoops, so she picks at random: brown for chocolate, and then pink – strawberry, that's safe. The scoop plunges in, clacking, scattering white flecks, drops of light. Her tongue reports, inevitably, the disgusting flavour of praline. She doesn't dare taste the other scoop, the pink one, which is trickling slowly down the cone; she no longer knows what to do about the big hollow in her chest, the ants gnawing at her heels, the all-consuming tension climbing her calves and invading all her space, there, along the seafront, dismembering the sky, the sea, the cliff, and the town shaped like a flight of stairs.

3

She's pleased to have found something so quickly. She'll have to hand in the keys at the beginning of July, when the seasonal lets begin, but she can return in mid-September, if she likes. The agency has a display of pictures of houses that look like holiday memories. Through the plate-glass window, she sees the waves, the beach, the ice-cream man out in sunshine that is already growing warm. The town is as hollow as a seashell, coiled up in the curls of the cliff. Here lets are by the week in summer; the seaside is like that. In the summer, the estate agent tells her, the population increases tenfold, and you should have seen the sea before the new water-treatment plant, for sewage, you understand. She sees the summer, the heat haze on the mountains, the windows swimming with blue reflections, the yellow light filling the town. The still air that gels like a mousse and grows hotter, flattening the sea, drawing the horizon closer, compressing the summer to the melting point. She sees the surfers, drawing the waves in their wake, a breath of cool air on the sand, and the children darting out from under the beach umbrellas, shouting in the white silence draped over the sunbathers like a sheet. She signs the papers. It's next door, a few yards to the left, an entrance hall with a tiled floor. With the keys she gets a complimentary kit containing packets of instant coffee, a small box of detergent, and some samples of sunblock. The samples have the same drawing of a house and family as the agency details.

They leave; he watches them through the front window. The little girl looks like a miniature version of her mother. They have the pale, slender bodies of visitors, the thin white arms, the ankles that look ready to snap. The subtle calm of the sea this morning masks the sound of their footsteps. Their faces make a bright mark, a nimbus that sails across the shop windows amid glints from the sea, the cars, the wristwatches of passers-by. An ice-cream's violent pink dribbles over the child's fingers, a stain chest high and growing ever larger, gleaming in the sunlight. Perhaps they're travelling. The father is in the harbour, on a yacht. There are some like that, every year, on their way round the world; they stop off to find work, and leave again three months later. While they're in town, they read to the children. They surf, drive around in vans, sail from place to place following the waves: California, Hawaii, Australia; they always end up passing through here.

Today there's hardly any swell. The sea heaves casually, sinks back without any energy, an elastic arterial pulsation; two hours from now will be low tide, at noon, with the sun at its zenith, and then everything will start all over again, the tide rising towards the old harbour, towards the casino, towards the blue shop window. At seven o'clock, when he lowers the blind, it will be high tide. He'll feel it behind him, close, peaceful, immense. He'll walk home along the cliff, where you can see further, breathe more freely. Now they're turning in to the entrance hall; he cranes his neck. She acknowledges him with a slight inclination of the head. Their hair melts in the light, a ray of sun has fallen on them, dissolving them; in their wake they leave wisps of hair that glow and are gone. Now they must be in the lift, which dispenses a synthetic strawberry scent to counteract the smell of tobacco every time its doors open; they reach the twelfth floor of the huge, ugly building, already past its best – which brought down the mayor and destroyed the seafront but has a lovely view. It's somewhere for her: he explained that to her, within the limits of the discretion inherent in his profession, inherent in the idea he has of his profession. For a single woman, for two people, or more (a studio flat – what does that mean? – ocean-going yachts are no bigger), it's somewhere you can find peace and quiet, gaze out across the sea, and immediately feel as if you're on holiday. It's fully furnished. He lives on the thirteenth floor, the top floor, and has a small balcony overlooking the cliffs: the building was constructed – this was the original justification – to shore up the cliff on one side. When you look on the map, it is a safe place to be in the event of a tidal wave, somewhere the sea cannot reach. Otherwise, you have to run up into the mountains. She shook his hand rather quickly when he tried to expand on his approach to the concept of accommodation. He'd like to write a book on the subject; for writing, a seascape is ideal. But all she cared about was the view. It's the desire for the view that motivates most clients.

The glass in the windows is so transparent that, before opening them, she hesitates, just for a moment, long enough to notice the almost invisible traces of raindrops, their mineral ghosts, or perhaps the salty traces of seaspray. She leans out; the sun hasn't reached them yet, they're obviously facing west, full western exposure overlooking the sea, so only the narrow gully in the cliff, where the Art Deco houses are collapsing, is getting any sun. It's hard to know where to look, how to decide: what's ending, what's beginning – the full side or the empty one; which piece of the planet borders the other, the blue subsidence of the sea, or the furnished heights of the town; whether the coast has given way before the waves, or the waves have found a berth, an anchorage here, as if the ocean's mass were holding on to the earth with only the wavering, weakened, repeated grip of its edge of lacy foam. The little girl hasn't finished her cornet, she's covered with dribbles, it's always the same with ice-cream. She sponges the child down at the sink, gives her a glass of water, then lets the water run until it's hot enough to make instant coffee. The unbreakable cups and glasses are decorated with the same seagull motif as the bedspreads. She pulls a chair over to the window; the sea clings to the beach, covering the sandy bed, the wrecks, the dead cities, and lingers on, settled and amnesic; a smooth blue mirror, so smooth and so blue it's hard to conceive of its depths: a shield burnished by a buffing wheel and curved at the periphery, delicately embossed with a hammer. Swimming ten strokes out from the shore, however, you would hover above the void, suspended, confident, thinking you could still just about touch the bottom, even though your body, seen from below, would no longer be anything more than a pale spectre silhouetted against a murky light, like the bell of a submerged church tower. There must be creatures down there, the child must have seen it on television, she knows all about that kind of thing: famous shipwrecks, whales like underwater cathedrals, sharks confusing surfers with seals (the surfboard is the body, the hands and feet are the flippers, and, bang, the water bleeds in the sunshine, and the washed-up surfboards have bites taken out of them, just like apples).

She is playing with the laces of her trainers, tying one bow, then another, then undoing them both and starting again. Her blisters have gone down. The wind comes softly through the window, a light morning breeze that ruffles the downy hair at her temples. They've been living in the flat for four days now. First they go and buy an ice-cream, then they sit outside the cake shop; her mother orders coffee, she drinks a glass of milk. They stay there for a long time. Schoolchildren go home for lunch; the owner of the cake shop lowers the awning against the sun. In the afternoon they walk along the shore. She's enrolled in the Blue Dolphins Club, which starts at four o'clock in the afternoon, and on Wednesday mornings at ten o'clock. In the evening they eat at the flat – pasta, cheese, and fruit – in the waning light that casts deep shadows around their eyes. Her mother chats, from balcony to balcony, with the man from the letting agency. At the end of the hall, beneath the sheets on the top bunk, she hears the zigzag of voices in the red night sky. They talk about the sea, the present calm and the phases of the moon, the high tides expected at the solstice (when the earth suddenly reverses the angle of tilt of its axis, big waves come rolling in), the imminent surfing championships, and the tourists who are beginning to arrive; her mother's voice becomes porous, purple, shot through with the last rays of the sun; the words slow down, elongate, coil up; she no longer hears the man's voice, she sees the sea and the surfers, the ice-cream man in his little van, the cliff exhaling mist in the white light. She curls up under the worn sheets, hugging the pillow. With one eye she can make out her mother, leaning on her elbows, her back and neck slightly twisted as she speaks to the terrace above. Her dress is ankle-length, and the light – a low, raking light – catches in the fabric: the material becomes violet, almost black, dotted with burning holes. The shoulder straps have disappeared in darkness. A tall triangular body, to all intents, with two arms and a head emerging from membranous flesh, floating in the breeze, a body with that voice, distant, detached, like a reply to words long gone: a hollow voice, warm, red. She feels her mother's hands in her hair: she's lying with her face buried in her lap. She's not crying any more. The sand glistens, the pines creak, the dune devours the forest; she hears the voice, back again, a deep voice that comes not from the throat but from the belly, she hears it through her nose, her eyes, her mouth, a voice that fills her whole body and wraps big nocturnal arms around her. She turns over, moves the sheet slightly aside; with her back to the night, her mother is looking at her. She instantly closes her eyes; she hears the rest of the sentence, a ripple in the phrase, a quick swerve: her father has gone off on a trip, whispers her mother. She thinks about the night, which will turn black; about the brilliant blue of the sea if she were to manage to escape, to find her satchel, to make a telephone call.

She sold the car to a garage in a seaside resort – the registration has given her away. The client agrees to give him an advance, he hangs up, opens an atlas. On the two-page two-dimensional representation of the globe, the sea is not that large, but it begins and ends everywhere. How do they decide that the seashore is *here*? Do they forget about boats, planes? Creatures appear between the continents: animals, monsters, some of those brawny horned beasts with the heaviness of fossils wrenched from the clay, stubborn, brutish, brow and muzzle pushing against the land mass. The Atlantic is an elephant, its trunk wound around Cuba, its tusks curved beneath Iceland. The Indian Ocean is a two-horned rhinoceros straining against Africa; from a certain angle, it's also an ancient camel, its humps flanking India. It takes some effort (the planisphere takes Europe as its centre) to see the Pacific, to piece it back together, rearing up against the earth: it's a bison, a yak, a buffalo, high in the withers; it gores China, tramples Tasmania, kicks at Tierra del Fuego. The paradox is that the continents are seals, whales, and manatees. He's known it since he was a boy. He trained himself early on to see the reverse of the planisphere; it's a healthy discipline, almost an ascesis, toning the optic nerves, the arteries and muscles; the abdominal wall tightens, the genitals retract; you must forget cities, plains, valleys, and look at gulfs as projections, harbours as bridgeheads, the surf as the edge of the world, and islands as abysses: then you see the blue, the shape of the blue. He closes the atlas, has a good stretch. He'll be going somewhere where there are waves. He'll rent a small flat and smoke on his balcony. In the evening he'll stroll around, read the paper outside a café, greet the regulars. He'll get to know the tide tables and which seasons are the best for fishing, he'll familiarize himself with the names of dangerous currents. He'll have an opinion on drift nets, on the demarcation of territorial waters. Reading the newspaper, he'll pay particular attention to the weather.

Occasionally a car goes by. It's three o'clock. The traffic light changes, imperturbable. The downstairs door lock buzzes. Her skirt is creased, her hair is sticking to her forehead and has lost some of its curl around her neck. The sun keeps battering the walls; the concrete makes a blinding gash in the bath of lime smoking against the sky. Her son-in-law woke her up with the name of a sea-side town. To see the sea – nothing could be easier; to see the sea, to hear it in a seashell – on this point, only some illness, or gross insensitivity, can paralyse the senses: the sky breaking up, the horizon, the clouds, and the tremendous expanse enlarging the view to encompass the world. She recognizes the name of the town, anyone would; a holiday town, with waves and swimming pools, trees, and villas glimpsed only as a section of wall, a red and white breach in the blue. She has seen reports on the news, received postcards, heard stories (Basques play pelota, sport berets, are blood group O-negative and have no earlobes, their language was spoken by the inhabitants of Atlantis, and they still bear the scars, below the mastoid bone, of what once were gills). She bends down, rubs her legs, rolling the hard balls of varicose veins beneath her skin. She closes her eyes; she longs to sleep all the time. Dreams bring her something of the child, a kind of sparkle, a colour, a way of imprinting the air, of altering the places where she's been. She would like to be sure she isn't getting confused – memories would be inappropriate here. It's her face that appears, a broad, pale halo, beaming, then solemn, the mouth, nose, smaller and smaller, she hasn't time enough to see, the town reclaims her, as if she were glimpsed through the portholes of a rocket as it takes off: the ground falling away, the periphery expanding as it empties, things sinking in the centre, dropping into the vortex of the centre, until they re-emerge (we're led to believe) on the other side – the red and white houses, the roofs that fold away, the streets that roll themselves up, the cliff that rises and wraps the beach up again, and the sea, even more vast and blue, overflowing into the town, into the sky; you pass through a curtain of clouds, and the town disappears, a mist, a great plain of white vapour, beyond which emerge, as a photograph from silver salts, lines, coasts, no longer beaches but a whole geography, bays, mountains, the spectacular curve of the Atlantic's coastline. The sea has filled all the space, the coasts have moved apart, then further still (the tectonic plates shift, the oceanic rift tears America from Europe, lumps of matter shoot up rhythmically from black deep-sea vents, confounding underwater Pompeiis and the devices of Captain Cousteau), the world turns blue, with two little skullcaps on the poles and a scattering of continents.

She opens her eyes; the flat is silent, dead of sunstroke. She feels her forehead, her cheeks: her face is puffy from the heat or sleep, a blur of lines on the window. Cars drive across her cheeks and her forehead is pocked by the windows on the other side of the street. The sun shimmers; dazzling flashes of light set things ablaze and obliterate them. The latticed balcony delicately divides the air into quivering squares. She gives up trying to work out what she is looking at; otherwise, everything giving way inside her will completely overwhelm her. The latticework keeps shifting position: drawing near, out of focus in the foreground, with disproportionately huge squares; or, on the contrary, slipping into the depths of the landscape, so that now the tree, the houses, the street, and the traffic light come closer, appear gigantic, with hazy outlines, sieved into millions of little cubes. The two views, foreground and distance, reverse; swap places; edges are both convex and concave, the perspective turns inside out. Watching science programmes on television – the life of atoms, anatomy, tectonic plates – she and the child were endlessly intrigued by that kind of difference: the two sides of the same world, the magma that supports the framework of the planet, flowing like a serum, organic, incredible, but most of the time invisible and hidden underground, beneath the familiar tarmac surface of streets, school playgrounds, public squares, car parks. The little girl's wonder at all this – she would like it to go on and on, to last like the perpetual flux of things – she'd like to continue fostering it, for as long as possible, but the bit of her brain that's still functioning warns her that she must leave right away.

She's learning to swim at the Blue Dolphins Club. The instructor's name is Patrick. First you duck your head under the water, and you breathe out through your mouth as you count to three. Then you hold the handrail at the side, you float on your tummy, and kick with your feet; finally you hang on to a long pole and let yourself be pulled along, puffing like a sea lion. This happens in the pool. You cross the promenade, go past the entrance to the casino and down some stairs. It's very hot; chlorine vapour, heavy with mildew, smells like stinking feet. The two other children learning to swim are Steve and Maïté. They leave their satchels in the changing room and eat snacks wrapped in aluminum foil. The changing-room floor feels damp underfoot; big cold drops fall from the ceiling. There always seems to be an iron bar banging against pipes or in the basement, each handle turned on the lockers clatters like forty metal doors, and voices sound as though they are echoing off armour plating, with cries and calls ringing sharply in the muggy air. The water makes her feel woozy. It tastes of salt. Maïté is crying, she says it makes her eyes sting. Steve says a pipe goes under the casino, pumping in sea water, sometimes sucking up a shark, and when it's the other way round, when the pool is being drained, they risk getting swept away to the bottom of a big pit inhabited by transparent fish. She ducks her head under the water; the water grips her hair and noises fill her brain. You sputter air, the outside world is a clatter of bubbles in the water; once you get used to it, you hear the forge beneath the cavern, the creaking of unseen chariots, the scraping metal of moving limbs and the crash of divers: the water parts, then flows together again, slowly, behind the body that emerges, smooth and glossy. When she has run out of air, she raises her head, and it's like a memory coming back to her: the matt quality of things, Patrick's clear voice, the bright sounds scattering between the vault and the surface of the water. Water is a great comforter, a hand held out beneath the body. You don't have to worry about the ground any more, keeping it at a distance, remembering your muscles and straightening your spine. You don't have to watch out, to stay awake. Water is like sleep. She no longer hears Maïté's sobs, or people's shouts, or Steve's stories. She lets go of the side, swims oblivious of the water, head submerged, body in motion and newly supple. When Patrick lifts her up at the end of the pole, she has grown the curves of a shell, and continues her crayfish siesta at the end of her fisherman's arm. Her mother helps her slip on her sweater, moving aside crayfish legs, folding back antennae as she talks to Patrick. They linger at the exit. She tries to hear what they're saying.

He hopes that, with the money from the sale of the car, she hasn't taken to the skies as he has, the two of them crossing, separated by the air, the fuselage, the void. He's in economy class, wondering how much he should charge his client. The plane is empty. The flight attendants are standing in the aisle, chatting. At the back of the plane, the din from the jet engines is so loud that he gives up trying to ask for another seat and lets the noise wash through him. The clouds have strange shapes, whites he's never seen before; the plane flies around them without leaving a whorl or a wrinkle in their suspended mass, as if a total silence on the other side of the window had made the vapour congeal. Frozen avalanches hang over the wings. Sculpting a gaseous geography, fortuitous in its freeze-frame, the air gilds the tops of the clouds; a delicate orange shadow holds them as if in the hollow of a hand. He shouts for someone to bring him a whisky. The attendant shows him how to use the bellpush. The clouds have vanished. He twists around in his seat, trying to glimpse, in the corner of the window, a last vertical slab of whiteness; he sees only his own face, layered by the triple-paned window. His eyes have an expression he hadn't known, that he wouldn't recognize in a photo, supposing that photos exist of such fugues: an expression that eludes his flesh and that he could not control from behind his face, a loss of mastery so complete – even though fleeting, stemming from memories of orgasm or childhood – that he hopes no one else caught sight of his reflection. The attendant takes the glass from his hand, gently raises the seat back and fold-down table, and motions to him, with a patient smile, to fasten his seat belt. For a second he fears she'll tuck a blanket around his legs; there's a faint odour of mint and the sanatorium about the plane. We have begun our descent, the pilot announces to the empty cabin, and we wish you a pleasant weekend. The coast is bright yellow alongside the green sea.

She has completely forgotten the satchel, it's gone, along with the car. The child's mouth is still open after asking the question, her eyes made ugly by an unpleasant fear. She would like to tell her that it's only a satchel, that they'll buy another. She touches the money in her pocket, the crackling thickness of new bills, a contact that brings an enormous sense of well-being. She looks for words, even one, to share this tranquillity with her, to invite her to look at the scenery, the beauty of sunlight on the sea, the surfers riding the solstice swell. She hesitates, taps the table between the coffee and the glass of milk. Now the child is going to cry; before that little foghorn sounds, she ought to take her on her lap, with hugs and promises, holding her so tightly she'd understand with relief where that small portion of space they must inhabit begins and ends. She places her hand on the child's; she feels, beneath her palm, a young rabbit sweating and trembling with a motionless anxiety, muscles rigid. She stands up to pay the bill, blinks, and the sunny sea clouds over like a sky. It's a flight of black spots, as fleeting as a dizzy spell. She thought, in the forest, that she'd lost her. She was only going to look at the sea, climb the dune and look at the sea. She returned; the tent was empty. Branches sliced through the darkness. The forest surrounded her. The sand fell away in shadow, quickly, beneath her steps. And then she saw her, an elf, among the black boles. She caught her, that fragile little body ready to melt in the night air, to dissolve in the surge of the forest; thought of swallowing her, reclaiming her; making her go back inside her womb, placing her arms inside her arms, her belly inside her belly, her head inside her skull. She leans for an instant on the back of the chair. The squeak of a pipistrelle fades from her hearing; sunshine returns to the sea and the cliff; the shadows retreat into their caves. The water rustles, twinkling as far as the eye can see with light: silver, green, and gold. She is stretched out under a tall poplar; she is in the fallen trees. A plane passes, tracing a white line where the sky is. It dips towards the earth, it's about to land, the jet engines overpower the sound of the waves.

Her eyes follow the shadowy cross gliding over the sea. She slept through most of the flight, it was the pilot's voice that woke her. Quickly she asks for another glass of champagne. She hasn't taken enough advantage of her first-class seat; she stretches her legs, rubs them, wipes her burning face with some graciously offered eau-de-Cologne. If she'd dared, she could have stretched out across the whole row of seats. The flight attendant has opened the curtains; the plane is almost empty. A postcard gleams below the window: a yellow beach, a white casino, a red luxury hotel; rows of beach huts; the sea cuts indentations, scooping out streets with two-toned façades. She should stay like this, in the air, with her forehead pressed against the window, and lift up every roof, shake every car, tip over every beach hut, and she would find them, she'd pluck them up between two fingers. The sea is green, flat, hammered like a sheet of copper; in the plane's shadow you can see through to the bottom, a long fish of seaweed and rocks, skimming over blue sands. The champagne is giving her a headache. She's got the hiccups, she opens the air-sickness bag but only retches. The plane banks; blood leaves her legs and pounds in her head.

Waves of humid air have entered the plane, bringing a peaceful, salty warmth. The flood of noise from the jet engines subsides. He grabs his hand luggage. The flight attendants in their blue caps say goodbye. He waits at the top of the passenger steps – in the wind, it's like a scene from a film – while a steward finishes helping an old woman with a red face. You have to disembark on to the tarmac and walk over to the terminal. He's as happy as a child. Some rabbits are sitting a little way away, hypnotized by the activity. Golfers are keeping a weather eye open at the far end of the runway, raking the sky with long drives borne aloft by the Alpine föhn.

4

He lowers the metal shutter, and the sun goes down with a grating sound; the white paint is flaking off, he'd better have a look at it. He puts on his dark glasses, takes a few steps back. His name is still clearly visible, dark grey in the lambent light. You have to try, every now and then, to look at things with a fresh eye. That's what he explains to his clients, so proud, most of them, of the house they're putting on the market. The buyer, he tells them, will notice the cracks, the roughcast chewed up by the sand, the dribbles of rust on the ironwork, the shutters pitted by the salt-air termites; especially buyers from inland, who come here to retire: those people fear the effect of the sea with a blinding terror. No one takes him seriously until a few months have gone by and the FOR SALE sign on the weather-beaten façade is itself beginning to flake off.

With the temperature rising, every evening he gets a craving for ice-cream. Cormorants dynamite the sea, each dive exploding a grenade of coolness on the metallic surface. He chats with Lopez, who has all the latest extras: now he offers syrups, toppings, you dip the ice-cream and it comes out coated in chocolate, you sprinkle on almonds or coconut; people like that. The wind from the south rattles the kiosk and stings the cheeks, bringing an oasis smell; the Sahara comes up here in gusts, blasts of nomadic sand; tomorrow the awnings, the door frames, the doorsteps will be ochre with this African dust. He hesitates for a long time before choosing his topping. Lopez shows him how to twirl the ice-cream in its cone, and the chocolate sets hard instantly. Just as he's about to decide on coconut, he senses their presence, the child and her mother, in front of the tubs. He'd like to say something witty, ask the ladies what they're having, but Lopez has beaten him to it, he knows that the child wants chocolate-coated strawberry, and the lady, nothing. He takes a thoughtful bite; later he will realize that neither the ice-cream nor the coating left any taste in his memory. The little girl's hair is full of sand, the downy strands around her forehead have stuck together in tiny clumps. As for her, she's still wearing her dress; never trousers, never a sweater. He suspects she washes her things every evening for the next day. The weather is on her side: an even temperature, mild, low humidity, thanks to the föhn. Her hipbones show beneath the blue fabric, stretching it across her stomach; the pleats drop smoothly in straight, deep folds that cover her ankles in shadow. She turns slightly away; the espadrilles point towards the sea, the knee creates a new fold, and the thigh, in the southerly wind, attracts a clinging swathe of fabric. He sees himself taking a step and feeling, almost absentmindedly, the point of her hipbone against his body. The child has called out. Her plastic sandals make a sound like suction cups on the stone slabs along the seafront. It's the guy from the beach club. He would now like, as a matter of urgency, to get rid of his ice-cream cornet. The black rubber of the wet suit encircles impeccably slender ankles, he's barefoot, and towers over them all by a head; he kisses mother and daughter on both cheeks. As for him, he shakes her hand, they say a few words about the influx of holiday-makers. Lopez is thrilled with the temperature, between 78 and 82 degrees, if it could just keep on like that, above 86 degrees and people don't want ice-cream. They wonder why. His cornet is melting stickily over his fingers, which have a sudden urge to wipe themselves on the dress billowing gently a few inches away. A strange calm has slowed the waves; voices cease; the sea falls silent. Light – a sunbeam – flashes across the child's face; he turns his head, he sees the section of cliff break off, five hundred yards away; he feels the bodies move closer together, the space between them set like plaster, from that one collapse, that one movement throughout the town: the cliff letting fall an immense vertical slab. The massive blocks sink into the sand without any explosion or spray of debris; it's after they've landed that they break up under their own weight, pieces shearing off suddenly, geometrical and yellow, leaving their edges sharp and new. Startled bats have swarmed out, catching fire in the sun. Then the sound rumbles, alien, penetrating.

The sea starts up again, and the cars; the taxi driver whistles admiringly as he drives on. A friend of his, who fishes down there, says that first you hear a gun-shot, that's the section pulling away; it has already fallen while you're seeing it still up there, held in place by the sound lag, and surprise. The chunk of cliff has left a gleaming golden gash in the living rock. He didn't see a thing. He was idly looking at the gutted houses, three columns on the edge of the drop, jagged with pins and open fractures; the columns are still there, it's a section of garden that fell. The beach is strewn with hydrangea petals, the aftermath of a party, swept away by waves.

He asks the driver if he can smoke, pulls the photo from his pocket. He plasters her to the window, where she passes by the houses, the beach, along the seafront, climbs a winding route up the side of the cliff. The bubbles of sunlight follow her. He questions the driver; no, he doesn't know her. His hotel room has a view of the sea, which he isn't obliged to tell the client, and anyway it's a good observation post. On the right is the lighthouse; on the left, the town. Just below, buttressing the cliff along with other modern buildings, a big, white, metallic hotel with a rigging of terraces and awnings is breathing with a noise like machinery. He wonders where she lives, and if she's thinking about the future.

To study the brown bears of the Canadian tundra, scientists stake out an area, not necessarily a very large one, and approach on foot. The only danger, in these zones near the pack ice, is stumbling across a fully awake polar bear. The brown bears, however, hibernate beneath the snow. So the scientists walk forward in a line – the way the army searches for bodies. Eventually someone feels, beneath the sole of his boot, snow that is softer, looser, snow that has been disturbed. Digging with his gloves, he uncovers a few chewed branches, beneath which black fur is snoring. The bear is given an injection to put it into a slightly deeper sleep; it barely twitches, a bee has stung it, up on a hive, it's gorging on honey, its adorable chops are quivering with pleasure. Then they study it, weigh it, stretch it out, tattoo it, they judge by touch its extraordinary powers of retention, they draw blood, analyse its tears, peer at its pensive eye. Certain sentimental researchers suggest a name; it's baptized, pawed over. The unique gentleness of this contact is hard to surrender; they all want to take it in their arms to put it back in its den. Now comes the most delicate part: the drying. All this handling has introduced snow under fur that is normally waterproof, so the sleeping bear risks catching pneumonia. The scientists have ordered little portable battery-powered hairdryers from Whirlpool. They form a circle around the bear in the buzzing of its dream beehive. The bear's fur steams, curls; now they put back the snow, with a happiness in their faces that is almost painful to see.

There's a knock on the door; it's the doctor, in his white coat with the striped monogram of the thalassotherapy clinic. He listens to her chest, palpates her abdomen. The scientists get back on their ski-mobiles and the sky grows dark over the tundra, as slanting rays of violet light skim crests of snow tinted orange. Rest is what you need, your pressure's a little low; did you see the cliff fall? He's scribbling down a treatment plan providing for a vitamin-enriched diet and revitalizing massages. What the Galapagos sea turtle subsists on is difficult to determine; the faeces are passed in the water, dissolving irretrievably into the sea. He takes the remote control from her hands, lowers the volume. It's the south wind that brings on headaches; your energy will return with exercise, I'm giving you this to help you sleep. A Franco-American team came up with the idea of attaching condoms to the turtles' shells to recover the excreta; the animals are hauled on board, she strains to hear the rest, they look like blocks of stone, with enormous fossilized eyes, and that's when the discovery was made (science advances crabwise, Fleming was studying moulds when he stumbled across penicillin) that seawater dissolves latex. The big, passive monsters dance in the turquoise water with the elegance of manta rays – then we cut daringly to bits of latex decomposing in greenish test tubes. The doctor has gone, leaving some complimentary chocolates in striped wrappers. Chewing, she leans against the wall as she goes out to the balcony. Now *there's* the answer to the problem of polluted seas, the supermarket bags (currently made of plastic) getting stuck in propellers, tangling fishing nets, clogging up the intestines of marine mammals, and

panicking moray eels into slicing one another to ribbons. The sound of the TV reaches her intermittently,
drowned out by the sea. The wind has fallen. The town
is disintegrating in the sun. A dense mist is rising, the
air is burning itself up, the sea and the walls are evaporating. The awnings of the thalassotherapy clinic ripple
softly, stripes above and below her grow taut, sag, and
the building flaps like a becalmed yacht. A yellow
smear marks the spot where the cliff gave way; she'd
had just time enough, while the luggage was being
taken care of, to perceive a general movement of collapse, as though the town were subsiding around the
fissure. The receptionists behind their counter, the bellboys, the porters, the lift operators, all froze, then
exploded into avid commentary, while she – she
remained facing the luggage, on the margin of what
was happening. She is lying in a deckchair; she needed
a blanket, in spite of the sunshine. Extra cushions were
brought to her, and a herbal tea with trace elements.
Tomorrow, as soon as possible, when she feels better,
she will begin looking for them.

The weather is changing. The haze remains, suspended,
blurring the mountains, pushing them back to the far
edge of the landscape, barely a mauve line halfway up a

sky of blotting-paper blue. The landscape has expanded, the air is swelling, the sea is rising, not in waves, but through a kind of internal depression, as if through the suction of an octopus backed up against the continent, in the troughs where the ocean begins. The moon has such an impact; on a very large scale (that of the hemispheres), you can observe, via satellite, the formation of a basin, a veritable crater: it's the moon driving away the water, fooling the forces of gravity, crushing the ocean in its centre and raising the tide (a physical phenomenon easy to observe: press in the centre of an unbaked tart crust, and the dough will climb up the sides of the tin). Then the moon catches its breath, inhales the atmosphere: the depression turns inside out and into a hummock, a cone, as the sea withdraws from its shores. At the times of greatest effect, equinox and solstice, the crater or the cone is so pronounced, each in turn, that the beaches are bared to the quick, long-forgotten boulders emerge, limpets are asphyxiated, and anemones dry out, until the tide floods in once again.

She ponders the stories Patrick tells her at the pool, wonders about the Great Siphon, which spins in the centre of the sea when the planet tilts on its axis, revolving in one direction or the other, depending on whether you're north or south of the equator. This evening, while brushing her teeth, she pulled out the plug to watch the little whirlpool; Patrick says that in Australia, where he plans to emigrate soon, the water flows in the opposite direction (and the moon shines upside down). Before her mother sent her off to bed she saw the weather map on TV, those big coiled masses whirring away at the slopes of the Earth. She awoke to a dark and windy night. The door slams between the studio and the corridor with the benches. Something like a residue of sun remains, red and scattered under the black sky. The flat is empty. There's a light on the thirteenth floor, in the neighbour's place. The fluorescent sea seems to have absorbed the day's energy and melted it into shining, lacquered waves. The sea rises and falls, slowly, unhurried, strong in its mass, full of octopuses, whales, hurricanes, shipwrecks, bestowing on the town the edge of its presence. It makes her feel grown up to be here, alone on the seashore; to stay here, at the precise place where land and sea come together. She's sitting in the chair her mother usually occupies; it's right next to the window, the balcony is too narrow. She's watching, waiting, she'd like to hear the voices. The studio glows faintly; the bed, the cupboard, the glasses left on the table seem softly lustrous, as if during her walks she had herself become so charged with sun that she now, like the sea, sheds her own light on the world. She tried to trace, on the weather map, the journey they had taken; she can recognize the place: at the bottom, to the left, in the curve, on the straight line of beaches, as easy to draw as a tightrope walker's wire. You balance there on one foot like a heron; past the seafront, you're already quite far from the delicate outline of the waves and it's hard to find the capital, inland, somewhere in the middle. She sees the flat, the flat where they live. On this side, the door to her parents' bedroom. On the other, the door to her bedroom. The bathroom at the end of the hall. The living room is deep, dark, broken up by brown hills, brighter corners, saturated with a kind of powder: the unchanged air has formed a sediment, fills the space, filters the glow from outside. The street lamps drape the windows in orange gauze. The rug is cut in two: in the light, the knights, the huts, the profiles with long hair; in the far end of the room, the real floral patterns, the semidarkness. She holds out her hands, feeling her way towards the familiarity of things, the sofa, the mirror on the mantelpiece, the four-legged table suckled by chairs, the big, squat lamp. The cracks in the floor tiles have got larger, crazing to form eyelids, ears, smiles, scattered over the ground. The dog's nose and the boar's snout are facing her, almost identical knots in the wood, on the doors of the sideboard. Her footsteps make no sound, she concentrates on breathing, on moving through the thick air. She recognizes the poplar at her bedroom window, and the clowns in a row, largest at one end, smallest at the other, wide awake on her pillow. When she returns, her father is sitting in the living room, he's in pyjamas but seems to have just come back from a trip. She runs to him; he appears to be asleep. His eyelids are closed but his eyes show through, bluish, translucent, without pupils, and in their depths she can still see him, his face upside down as in the back of a tiny spoon. It's the terror that wakes her up. The french window creaks, for a second she doesn't understand, and the sea tosses beneath the windows back home: the waves break where the poplar whispered, rolling in at the foot of the block of flats, licking the old railings, spitting salt spray on the entry-phone numbers. Then it's like waking up for a second time, the feeling of being put back in place, of knowing once more exactly where she is: here, in front of the sea, at the interface of the world. She climbs the stairs to the flat of the man on the thirteenth floor. The staircase is rough concrete, bare beneath the small orange light. Sometimes the building shakes, you'd think it was the

waves breaking, but it's the lift: the machinery makes
the weights oscillate in the shafts. The man seems surprised. Her mother is not at his place. She accepts an
ice-cream, not a good ice-cream, a watery one. You can
hear the waves and the lift alternately as if, on the top
floor, the building's two arcs intersect: the pendulum of
the machinery, the to-and-fro of the sea. He asks her
where her mother is. She sees the telephone number,
written in her head, learned by heart along with the
prohibition against accepting sweets: you are lost, kid-
napped, you've been discovered on the other side of the
country, somebody's hurt you, you went to the wrong
school, got on the wrong underground train, you fell ill
far from home. But the image immediately goes dark,
like an unplugged TV. She moves away from the screen
for a moment, steps back a few feet, then moves closer
as if surprised, with her eyes wide open – but there's
nothing where what she learned by heart should be,
nothing but a hole that goes on for ever. She looks for
lines, sounds, an echo (but there's no word on the tip of
her tongue, only a hint of a rhythm, ten digits, all possible). She sees her father get up, however, knocking
over an object that blocks his way, and search through
the accumulating shadows for a telephone he cannot
find. He stands there, pale, frightened. Darkness sur-

rounds him, slowly reclaims him, he calls out, the dust motes whirl around, shadows erase him, consume him, and she loses him in the shifting of the furniture, in the incoherent night, as if she were peering into troubled water, through which drifts to the surface, from freshly disturbed algae, a turbid cloud shaped like a seahorse. The man has stood up; the sea is getting impatient, throwing handfuls of water at the windows; he stays out on the balcony, leaning on the rail. The rain begins to plaster down his hair. The top of his shirt darkens, his trousers stick to his buttocks, drops of water cling to the edge of his jaw.

He wipes a hand across his face, grips the rail; the iron is wet, gritty to the touch. The weather has suddenly changed. The bistro owners bring in their tables, the windows are steamed up, the different muffled musics sputter in the storm; it's probably those lights – blurry and perhaps more festive like that, facing the wilderness of waves – that distress him so, as though he were a castaway. The range of possibilities is not huge: the bars on the beach, or along the main street; unless he took her straight to his place, up on the cliff, where the surfers hang out. The rain is winding down, the kid is watching him through the pane of glass blistered with drops of water and light, but he'll be perfect in his assigned role: the babysitter with ice-cream in the freezer.

The cormorants are asleep, gothic and black in the lighthouse beam. Tourists are leaving the Corsaire, the port is deserted, the tarmac glistens. The cormorant is a seabird with permeable feathers, obliged to dry out between dives, wings stretched like an umbrella. She hangs on Patrick's arm, laughing at random; she's never sure if he's joking or not. Through the misted-up window of the bistro they've entered she sees the tall block of flats, locates the studio flat thanks to the neighbour's light, above and to the right; she'll stay another five minutes. Every night the façade is brighter and brighter, as more and more flats are occupied. When she arrived, the neighbour was like a lighthouse keeper, alone on his balcony, perched there like a bird. In less than two weeks she is supposed to leave; by then the building will have illuminated all its units, like an Advent calendar for July. She runs her fingers through her hair, chasing the idea away. She's conscious of Patrick's gaze, of her taut shoulder straps, the curve of her breasts beneath the fabric, her bare armpit. She says yes to another beer, and after that she's going to leave. The bar is warm, humid, with a smell mingling tobacco and seaweed; the table at which they finally sit is covered with a film of salt and water. She's given a plate; Patrick has ordered an assortment of local specialities for her, he knows the owner, they grab each other by the arms, laughing. The ham tastes like an old handbag. Patrick clinks glasses with her; she smiles at him, bends her neck, her hair falls forward. She feels she's confusing (and perhaps that's it, suddenly, that urgency) the desire to lock his masculine hips between her thighs with the desire to be alone, alone with her breasts, her skin, her hands. Shiny with wear, her dress is as damp as her face, not from sweat but from steam. The door is ajar; a cool draught sometimes wafts by her knees. She should go home, but the sound of the sea and that heavy marine humidity make it seem that nothing could happen, that no one could ever be left entirely alone here. He takes her outside and into his arms on the top of the cliff. She can see the roof of the big block of flats, it seems to hold sway over the entire town. His saliva is salty. Their cheeks stick together, their hair sparkles with water droplets. She loves this numbness, the lips obliterated by the crush of contact, the face that grows full, melts into the body, which turns round as the mouth descends, sinks in, embeds itself in the flesh while the limbs, multiplied and curved, fall back around a centre growing more and more intense. The octopus, hunting the spiny lobster among the rocks it calls home, glues itself in a star shape over the crevice; its large head can be seen swaying in the current above a patiently waiting mouth. Trapped, the spiny lobster waits, until hunger makes it careless. It tries to leave; the beak strikes between head and thorax, at a joint in the carapace, paralysing the victim alive within its shell, which is sucked clean, to the exasperation of the under-water fishermen with their spears. They walk along; she likes the space he leaves between them, the wet asphalt, the intermittent flash of the lighthouse, the great hori-zontal sweep that soars across the face of the town. The tops of the tamarisks appear and disappear, tangled against the sky and then plucked back by the cliff. From time to time she draws closer and Patrick slows down; the light is so intense that both of them stagger when the beam hits them, as though a third body were hugging them. She can make out, in its glare, the texture of his skin, the pores finely embroidered by the salt and the sun. The days are so long, she's seeing the night for the first time, a night in June, so short that she can't wait. He rings a doorbell, their bodies flicker in the beam before the door opens on to a hallway, people, music and lights; they're in a club, not at his place at all. She hadn't listened to a thing he was saying. He kisses some girls, squeezes some shoulders, shakes hands across the bar. Guys are laughing, leaning back, they have the same yellow hair as Patrick, the same knotty forearms, the same loose, brightly coloured clothing. The music pounds in your chest. Two very young girls are dancing in very short skirts; smoke rises peacefully through the lights, winding around their childish hips, lazily encircling the glitter balls. There are some lycée students sitting next to her, they roll a joint, hold it out to her, shout a question; probably: where is she from? Or else: how long has she known Patrick? She looks around for him, he waves to her, his teeth are ridiculously white in the ultra-violet light, and the contour of his neck, below his perfect jaw line, is enough to make you scream. He's bent tenderly over some guy, yelling in his ear, it must be surfer talk, English terms for various waves and surf-board manoeuvres. She stands up; a cool mist floats around one group; that's where the door is. The sea is fresh, incisive. Her ears are ringing; each wave rolls in there and breaks, wresting her free. She walks through the tamarisks, down the cliff, down the narrow old-fashioned steps. The fake wood is so old that the iron shows through the moulded handrails: long, bare tendons, red and salt-corroded in their concrete bark.

The building's bulk takes her by surprise, looming up blackly, cutting off a flight of fancy on the steps: one of those terraces where, ever so long ago, crinolines crowned by parasols were allowed out in the sun. A modern platform of lightweight steel is grafted on to the amputated terrace and winds at length around the building. It's a kind of scaffolding, emergency stairs for a major disaster; she has already explored them in daylight with the child, suspended in the sky, discovering what's on the other side of the building where they live. The birdshit makes it a bit slippery, sometimes you disturb a few birds. The seafront below seems narrow through the tiny gaps in the metal floor; the sea rolls beneath her feet. The waves advance, line after line of them, rounded towards the opposite curve of the beach, so that from above it looks like a huge X, a hyperbola, and you wonder how the join is made, or what extraordinary passages are opening up between the water and the world. The sky is a silvery black, glinting with clouds. A plane flies by, the last plane of the evening, the connection for transatlantic flights. The rain is advancing, as though the sky were drawing nearer, wrapping its density into a great fold that constantly shakes free, rippling and shuddering; the squall comes ever closer, stirred up in the bottom of a colossal cauldron, making visible the invisible: wind, air. Now she hears the noise, the boiling and hissing, a hundred thousand live coals heating the sea and raising gusts of wind. The waves have become mute things crushed by the tide above, you see the edge coming on, you see the foaming sky. She braces herself in readiness. The wave passes over her, in one second she's drenched, slammed up against the wall by the shock. Access to the balconies is barred, she has to retrace her steps. She can make out the tamarisks, thick with shadows; she moves quickly, dripping, out of breath. The metallic clang of her foot-steps is immediately absorbed by the squall. She's beginning to feel cold. With the dense, brutal rain the night has become completely black, booming and thun-derous. She runs her hand along the rail, feels the steps beneath her feet; no light at all breaks through any more, only a strange softness – swift, periodic – arrives at moments to slow down the wind – probably the remnants of the lighthouse's glory. A streaming claw strikes her face; she has found the trees again, and the cliff. The little stairway is a cascade of muddy water. She leans against the tree trunks. She can't see a thing any more, not behind her, not over by the block of flats, not under the trees in the din of the rain, in that forest growing – black and crackling – from the firestorm of the sea. Someone is there. Someone is waiting for her beneath the leaves. She sees him now, she can make out the bright circle of his face, the dark line of the shoulders, the white fists. It's him. Her heart stops. He takes her by the elbow; she feels the cold, wet fingers, she has no excuse, a husband, a father, it's all there, she has to follow him. He asks her where she's been; he's been looking everywhere for her. She's laughing now, she abandons herself to the oblivion of those arms: let him carry her off, let him take her. It's Patrick. For the first time he asks questions. Back at his place he talks to her about Australia, Wollongong, Twofold Bay, he has friends over there, he's going. They laugh: that's a lot of water to cross. Their hair has dried, he puts down his glass, he comes over. Afterwards, she will get dressed again, he will pick up his sentence where he left off; his blue irises will twinkle like a deodorant advert. Perhaps he'll suggest she comes to Australia. Behind the town the clouds will have whitened, though the waves will still be black; the night will withdraw, cold and west-bound, to the bottom of the sea, leaving pale seaweed beached beneath the sky; she will walk, slowly, skirting with dreamy steps the immense absence of the sea.

5

There aren't many people at the beach yet. He jogs down to get as close as possible to the waves, spreads out the towel from his hotel, and goes right into the water. The trunks he brought with him were so old that when he put them on the elastic gave way, crumbling like parchment; he had to buy a new pair at the local Galeries Lafayette. The water is freezing; he feels like squealing, he hops from one foot to the other; with each little jump the cold slashes at his ankles. Great waves break a yard away, folding the horizon over, pulling it across the sand, dragging long streaks of bright sky in their wake, regathering their strength, rearing up again and again. He proceeds with caution, watching for that very brief moment as each wave catches the sun: just beneath the crest, before it rolls over. A turquoise transparency, precious, fleeting, immediately swept away. He's in up to his knees, the current pulls first one way, then the other; the sea in that spot is white with darting green patches. A few swimmers slip between two waves and resurface with ease further out, beyond the boiling surf, laughing crazily. In one swoop the universe turns upside-down, the beach pounces on him, the sky coils upwards, a skin splits, sloughed like a glove turned inside out: space has caved in at the centre, releasing a gastric cannibal juice – he's being tasted, something is trying to ingest him, but finally the breakers vomit him up. The sand of the depths has left a long red weal on his belly; it's a bit too rough hereabouts. He laughs all alone, hiccuping; a colony of sea urchins has moved into his sinuses, he coughs and spits, and spies a kind of gigantic puddle where he can discreetly jettison the sand now weighing down his trunks.

The sun has come to rest here, on this smooth surface; the water is deep, calm, and warm. He wiggles his toes, very white in the limpid water, detached from his feet, zigzagging next to his calves, his thighs jutting from his stomach, midriff overhanging various scattered parts. He closes his eyes, basks. The round mass of water sways, gently pressing his body; he floats unaided, leaning against the water, in its delicate motion; he is part of the beach, the sea, and everything swaying in the sea. He is drifting off to sleep, in the hum of jostling waves, with a little way away swimmers screeching like seagulls, but something stays him on the edge of slumber; something like a memory, a tiny anxiety. In the dream which is just beginning to establish itself, still moored to the morning by the blue of the sea, the yellow of the beach, the fancy red hotel, he sees the lighthouse, pointing distinctly, a cylinder so bright it throbs and vibrates in broad daylight: three, four, five lighthouses against the thunderstruck sky. The swimmers' cries draw a new shrillness from the waves, a harsh, eddying note; he breathes underwater, astonished but unafraid, he sees the waves curling upside down, in the brief green light: the cloud cover rising, exploding outwards, overflowing, drawn by a sudden force pulling on the top of the world. The whistling persists, grows louder, brings him back to shore. He opens his eyes; a guy in red trunks is gesturing at the edge of the pool. Lifeguard, it's written across his chest. He rights himself awkwardly. The air feels icy. The guy is talking to him about still waters, deceptive, eel-like currents, especially one called the *baïne* that captures, drowns, destroys, sluicing out pockets of water as if pulling a plug. Meekly, he complies. He has always hated cops.

They are to meet as the tide comes in for her first swim in the sea. She's early, bending over the shallow pools among the rocks. Her mother has been renting a beach hut and a deckchair for the past few days; she bought a pretty swimsuit, a scarf she ties around her hair, and some large dark glasses; she smokes, she smiles at her; she's so pretty that looking at her too long almost makes your heart ache. The rock pools are sheets of glass, windows on the world below: you see how crabs sidle across tiny deserts; how for no apparent reason translucent shrimp, perched on canyons, frolic with leaps and jumps that contract their intestines, straight lines on to which are slipped seven rings of aqueous flesh; how periwinkles roll to the foot of silt screes and, all in a dither, readjust their opercula; how astonishing, frightening, and easy it is to dare dip in a finger and quite pointlessly bring disaster to this world. Her mother is still there, in the deckchair; she has tipped back her head. Behind her dark glasses her eyes are sure to be closed; her face is unclouded, blind, welcoming the sun, like an open hand, a face from which all shadow, without exception, has fled to crowd into the hollow between her breasts. On the sleek body, shown to advantage by the swimsuit, there is no longer anything but this dark triangle, this eye-catching medallion that makes her visible, recognizable, and disturbing above all other women. A few sea urchins with air bubbles pearling among their spines keep watch underwater:

stern, suspicious, inaccessible. The anemones are viscous, shutting savagely at a touch: lightly grazing their long fluorescent lashes makes them retract behind their red eyelids, after which you must wait, as patiently as possible, for something in there to decide, or to forget, and for these big empty eyes to open wide again under the sea. She checks, her mother is still there in the canvas chair; simply by running a few steps she could be immediately beside her: vacant, fathomless, laid out flat on her back by the sun. She sprinkles water over the fine crust of shells on a dried-out rock, and they open like magic squares, spitting and effervescing, trusting in the rising tide. She glances around; no one, including her mother, is watching her. She tramples the anemones, it's harder than she'd thought, the sole of her shoe slips off them, rubber on rubber. There's nothing inside, just this flayed muscle, no eyelashes, no light, not even squished guts. Big empty shells have bleached around the rock-pool like bones; they look like souvenirs, heavy in the hand, like stones; grandmother had some at home, you could hear the sea inside. She sticks a finger in the water, scattering her reflection; then the circles close up again, a very fine dust settles to the bottom, and her face comes back together: her eyes, nose, mouth, reunited on the jelly of the water. She returns slowly across the sand;

her mother has sat up in the chair and is talking to Patrick.

She was woken by the arrival of breakfast, brought by a chambermaid, or a nurse, in a blue-striped overall. She used to rise with the sun, and now she is as if possessed by sleep. On the bedside table, she has placed a framed photo of the child, the same one she had on the television. She sips a little coffee, nibbles on a croissant. Something in her body is crushing her, restraining her; she's like a heavy beast that's been sleeping, curled around itself, for several days. In the summer, when there's no school, and the child has been dropped off early in the morning by her mother before work, they take a train to the forest. They order lemonades at the refreshment stands; pushchairs and children's scooters arrive from the smart suburbs bordering on the woodland; climbers in rubber-soled shoes silently overtake them, heading for rock faces to which they will cling with their long spider-monkey arms. Further along, on a slab of limestone, they eat cubes of cheese and apples cut into quarters. The sun spreads out in the vapour exhaled by the foliage; the world is enveloped in a fleecy pillowcase, pale yellow, overwhelming the black tree trunks, erasing branches, rubbing out paths; the two of them bathe in this softness, in this woolly air where the sunbeams melt together, swelling with the pressure of the day. The wind, slowly, passes by. The capped earth pillars, the White Lady, the tall rock chimneys glide above the trees. The shouts of children reach them from very far away, through the thick milt of light. The forest is silent; the birds prefer the clearings. The two of them are fascinated by the presence of fossils on the flat faces of stones: spirals, little chiselled chambers, the valvules of vanished shells. The sea receded, the mud caught them in its matrix, and their flesh was consumed, leaving behind, as humus for the primeval undergrowth, only the impression of their passage. She explains to the child that it's here that the city was built, in the quarries, its walls the archives of the sea, sliced up by the stonecutters. In the streets, on the way home, they keep an eye out for the coiled shells of ammonites, and the lines drawn beneath the porches, with dates, to mark the extent of the floods. From the woods to the city, the afternoon accompanies them with a seamless light along the deserted streets, a light as warm and raspy as a voice. The child, in the photo, has that tanned summer look. She had just come back from the mountains, she'd never seen the sea. He used to say it was healthier, quieter, less touristy in the mountains. She tried to show her the sea, in the woods, from the top of the White Lady, where nothing protects the branches from the sun, where everything – the foliage, all the varieties of trees, even the clearings – blends together and flattens out in the glare. Then the sea appears, so vast that the curvature of the Earth becomes apparent. The child smiles, holding her hand. Television gave her the general idea, while the forest shows her the movement, and the wind, space, froth and pollen suggest the swell. She breathes, drinks, enjoys herself gazing at the phantom sea.

That photo – she took it herself. The child has a far-away look, seems slightly disorientated; back in the city, parents at work; talking only grudgingly about the trip, not saying exactly what she wants. The two of them had returned to their routine. There were ten days left before the start of term, time enough to make sure she still knew how to read and write, time to go back to the forest. Iridium is a white metal from outer space; its presence on Earth is due only to the chance falling of stars. There is one stratum, sometimes visible on the surface, that contains these nuggets with the rainbow name. Above this iridized stratum, there are no fossils of dinosaurs, which is the main plank in the thesis that their disappearance was due to a meteorite. In the afternoon, tired from their walks, falling asleep on the sofa, she and the child watched them collapse on television under a black sun, as ash from the meteorite, mingling with dust from the impact, slowly buried their death throes. They went to visit them, in the museum, on rainy days. The child trotted, tiny and well informed, among the big bodies frozen in mid-stride, among their claws, teeth, feet, among those impossible cold-blooded machines with eye sockets larger than the human skull, and yet she was merry, self-assured, walking jauntily by stone skeletons in dioramas, where the duck-headed iguanodon wades around on two hind legs in what will become a forest. The child knew all about absences, they didn't faze her, but she would stop, dumbfounded, in front of the jars of foetuses. And as for her, she would discover old memories, an ancient trust in things; she saw herself again, accepting these marvels, and she was proud of bequeathing them, of participating, persevering after death, still giving life to the child, since through this boundless legacy she would never cease to belong to her. From her bed, she gazes out across the balcony at the spectacle of the denuded ground, torn open through its geological strata: the petrified sapwood of the cliff, where the Earth, like an old tree, inscribes time circle by circle. The hotel's own television channel explains the benefits of thalassotherapy: long, lithe bodies luxuriate in various saline muds and then stretch out, coated and cosseted, in impeccable white dressing-gowns. The masseuse is waiting to wrap her in seaweed. Apparently she will be staying there a very long time, floating in sargasso, unable to leave the room and the cliff.

'Here we go': that's all he can think. He twists the photo this way and that in his fingers; he doesn't really get it: this guy, with wet hair, in Bermuda shorts with Day-Glo stripes, who has pulled the photo out of a Galeries Lafayette bag bulging with a sandy towel – it doesn't make any sense to ask him if he's with the police. Has he questioned other agencies, the hotels? When he tries to give back the photo, the guy keeps hold of his arm. It can't be her husband. A husband would seem less calm and would be better dressed. 'Take another look,' says the guy. She's three-quarter face, summery, her hair loose; it's a picture that doesn't tell him anything, a picture of the light around her, of the space she occupies, of the lines of her face. It's hard to make out her surroundings, blurred by the wind and her hair; leaves, perhaps. Where is it? What has she done? What merits an inquiry like this? He'd like to see a photo of her house, her husband, her dog, her parents; a photo of her in winter, in autumn; one of her childhood, her school. He'd like to see a photo of her when she's old, and when she's gone. He'd like to see her making love. He'd like to see her crying, raging, suffering. He'd like to see her change over time. If this guy here, sitting in front of him, were a rep for a company offering a rather specialized service, he'd immediately sign a contract guaranteeing him, for life, news of her, pictures of her, through clairvoyance or omnipresence. Frightened, finally showing some emotion, she hastily gathers up her belongings: that swimsuit she just bought, her scarf, the child's bits and pieces – without a word for him, of course, without a thank you, but running to the door he points out to her and then opens for her, following him down the fire escape on the side of the building; the walls are vibrating, the guy's about to get out of the lift, he warned them in the nick of time. Then, the car, he will have rented a car. They'll head south, they'll take the ferry at the tip of the continent. The guy has stood up, he takes back the photo, leaves the number of his mobile. In three days, at most, he'll have realized that the only place to hang out in the town, its centre, where everything happens, is the beach: he'll see her, he'll recognize her, sitting there, idiotically, while the kid plays a few yards away with their pet surfer. He will compare her features with the face in the photo and discover no difference between them. He's outside now, pretending to read the notices in the window, unless he's enjoying the sun, hands in the pockets of his Bermuda shorts. He doesn't want to detain him. He'd like simply to give her the message, let her know what he's done for her, that he's kept quiet about her, just like that, expecting nothing. After all, she hasn't paid the rent for June yet; he could evict her now, it's almost July.

With the ten thousand francs from the savings account plus, let's say, fifteen thousand from the sale of the car, ten thousand if she didn't get a good deal, from which you subtract two months' rent for her bolthole; assuming she's paying three thousand francs a month, she can hold out all summer, unless she's had to switch to a weekly let, which begins, according to a small notice below the display window, on 1 July. He finds it easy to picture her in the décor of the show flat, drinking tea between the yellow curtains, overlooking the blue sea; or in the garden of that house, calling the dog, getting ready to meet a smiling husband carrying a child on his shoulders. Two million for a house; he's not likely to move here in the foreseeable future. The nylon fabric of his trunks is already dry, and he can feel the sun through his T-shirt. He'll treat himself to an ice-cream. The guy in the letting agency is pretending to read a file; he knows that woman so well he couldn't think of anything else during the entire interview, just like the way alcoholics, in the middle of a conversation, can't help following the bartender with their eyes. The ice-cream man knows her too, no question. He shakes his plastic bag, blows sand off the photo. He could spend some time here, with his wife's photo. A widower, alone – people would whisper a few discreet words behind his back. He'd have the right to stay there by the sea. It's 81 degrees. The sun is taking up all the space. The ice-cream man is talking about the lovely weather and the ideal temperature for business. His name is Lopez. He's only got a top half, in a little kiosk. He watches the tide come in, go out. He must know the extreme range of the equinoxes, the level the water can reach by stretching or contracting, like a big muscle. He must know on which day, and at which hour, such-and-such a rock emerges or vanishes, he must have noticed tendencies, inclinations, long periods of time when the sea is greyer, greener, choppy or with a swell on it, dull or sparkling, beneath a sky that lets more or less daylight slip through. Or else the sea is only a back-ground, the verso of the town, a given as elementary as a clement temperature for the ice-cream trade, a bit of blue glimpsed between people's heads on sunny, crowded days, while Lopez waits for the winter months in order to regain the use of his legs.

He is sitting on a bench, enjoying his ice-cream. Lopez is leaning forward unobtrusively, watching him. He's in no hurry. The promenade is well policed. He'll be able to ask all the questions he wants, of Lopez, the lighthouse-keeper, the lifeguards, the tea-room waiters, the fishermen, the man who rents out beach huts and deckchairs. Few places in the world are scanned by so many eyes. It's almost a surprise, a slight deception, not to find in the photo any complicity, any shared aware-ness of this place, limpid and identifiable. The locks of hair are immobilized in the light; she's a woman who doesn't know a thing, who isn't planning to go any-where, who'd never imagine a break-up, absence, kid-napping. The wisps of hair hover motionless around her. She's risking prison for child abduction, not to mention losing her identity if she keeps on running, but you won't see it in her face. He'll run into her, she'll glide by him, in that sunny seaside oblivion, in the light in the photograph. He looks up; people are strolling, roller-blading, walking dogs, chatting. He had thought, for a moment, that he was alone. But he knows them all.

They could all recognize her, all confirm the absolute reality of that face.

Yesterday, trying on swimsuits in the Galeries Lafayette, she was startled by the suntan she saw in the mirror: two slender white lines crossed on her back, pale legs, very brown arms; her hair is blonder; her palms, contrasted with the darker skin of the backs of her hands, are as pink as the inside of a seashell, while the heels of her tanned feet are orange, polished by the sand. She doesn't understand how she could have bronzed so quickly. Being careful with the protective strip in the crotch of the new swimsuits has reminded her that she has her period, that she'd made an appointment, she seems to recall, for some time in June, a routine check-up. She leans back against the mirror, which feels cold; it's pleasant in the store. The child is playing at being a ghost with the changing-room curtains. Standing with her legs planted wide apart, she sees that her thighs are thinner, veined with pink and blue, soft – especially near her genitals – from being concealed so long beneath the dress, while the tanned skin of her arms, shoulders, and back is coarser. She leans against the rear wall of the cubicle for a moment, crumpling a bathing suit in her hands, calm, astonished to be so alone, so feather-light, immortal. Now, as she lies in the deckchair, areas left pale by the dress can be seen beneath the straps of the new swimsuit, especially just above her breasts, where she's turning pink, but the dividing line will soon be gone. The sun goes through the skin, deliciously warming and dilating the lungs and other organs; she has a vague recollection – she's heard it somewhere – that tubercular patients used to sunbathe like this, in reclining chairs, on balconies overlooking the sea, even in winter, tucked up in elegant tartan rugs, chatting desultorily, immensely weary, and with a book that was always too heavy just about to fall from their hands. Apparently the winter here is rainy, which supposedly explains why the countryside inland is so green. Consumptives preferred the Mediterranean, oleanders, the scent of almond and orange blossom. She hunts for the sunblock in the bottom of the Galeries Lafayette bag. There's some fruit for the child, a sweater in case she gets chilly after her swim, a large towel brought from the flat, and the English grammar she borrowed from Patrick's place, along with a Walkman that he obviously didn't use. With a half-decent memory, it doesn't take long for your English to come back.

They've come to fetch her from her balcony for her seaweed massage. She was watching the mirages out at sea, the islands born of the sunlight's vibrations, rather like bouquets, balancing on a single stem, that blossom into broad shadows just above the horizon. Just as it's difficult, in foggy weather, to know whether it's a mountain range stretching far out to sea or whether it's a cloud, solidly sculpted, mimicking a lofty peak, similarly she no longer knows if the islands exist, blurred by the light, or, if the ocean is uninterrupted between here and America, that a distant West is throwing its mirages up over the Earth's rim. Perhaps the planet has veered off its axis, bowing its blue head towards the sun; the magma has shifted, throwing gravity off centre and skewing the rotations of the Earth, which lists and pitches like a freighter under the weight of its own cargo. They hoist her out of her reclining chair. She resists; there's a group of children on the beach, she wants to watch; they tell her it's the season for school trips, that she must snap out of her lethargy, get herself moving, take part in activities, they won't be bringing her meals up to her room any more. She falls asleep in the bath; the seaweed unravels in the heated saltwater, cooking, thickening; she no longer feels her legs under the long slimy ribbons, her hands are corals, her arms dead eels, and her breasts moonfish that float, slackly, beneath the drifting net of her skin. The mermaid is a mythological animal familiar to all cultures: half woman, half fish, or sometimes half bird; skin, hair, scales, or feathers; enchantress or victim, sliced in half, quartered, cleft by desire. Christopher Columbus's sailors confused her with the manatees of the grassy deltas of the Indies; the females have breasts and broad, welded thighs. The human race seeks an accommodation between walking upright (hands free, narrow pelvis) and childbearing (wide pelvis); quadrupeds give birth quickly, without suffering, and sirens are born on the bosom of the waves. If she had it all to do again, she'd happily make the same mistake and ask once more for legs. Her thoughts are in a whirl, maybe she's getting senile. And yet, she's been doing mnemonic exercises for a long time now: she learns verses, lists, revisits the museums of her youth room by room. In her son-in-law's presence, she was able to reconstruct that entire last afternoon spent with the child, up to her daughter's arrival, the blue dress with the crossed straps, and that position, the body standing limply at the sink, the thin stream of water; she could remember the precise angle of the sunlight striking the tiled floor, and the back of that neck, through which no command, no impulse seemed to move. But she hasn't come up with a single useful detail, a word she might have said, a wish, a curse, something out of the ordinary, anything at all to help the investigation; she didn't know what to tell her son-in-law, how to describe the vacancy of the body, and that light, so intense it seemed to flicker; what was needed was a photo, a photo of her memory, a beam shining through her skull and projecting her recollections on to a screen. Her legs seem to have melted under their own weight, her body has leaked away; she tries to open her eyes and there's nothing any more but that gelatinous, lukewarm sensation, what amnesiacs must find instead of memory itself. Still, she'd be able to remember everything, the living and the dead, bring back forms striding along, set houses upright, recall words, until that specific episode, that parenthesis, that gap; she'd need only to stop, choose a time frame, identify a case, grasp the essentials and understand, but everything streams past, flowing along, and suffering bobs about like a cork. They're lifting her up again, she feels a pain beneath her ribs, the light is green, rippling, as in an aquarium, the Museum of the Sea is, along with the cliff, the jewel of the town, turtles, octopuses, seahorses, red sea bream, seals from the ocean that were sick or caught in nets, sharks in fine fettle flown in from Florida. She's cold, she must be out of the seaweed.

She'd like to pull herself together again, put back her arms, legs; she sees a hand, her smooth and slender hand, her smooth and slender legs, her light, round breasts, that remembered body that could also wear elegantly, on the same young shoulders, blue dresses with crossed straps. That's how the child will grow up: tall, thin, as though fathers had no effect on this lineage of square hips, small breasts. She'd like to move but bits of her life are stirring, sluggishly, tingling faintly: childhood in the hollow of her hand, adolescence in the bend of her arm, adulthood in faint jolts in her chest cavity. Memories are dismembering her, it's this disease that's attacking her – the one that, far from drying up her memory and its images, is making a tumour of time where her body ought to be.

6

He calls the client. He tells him, basically, the truth: that he's on the right track, that she's here. He doesn't go into detail, talks about the climate, the implications of being in another country, mentions witnesses; he asks for a little more time, and in particular for the precise instructions that get clarified only at the end: what does he want, exactly? The client says he wants the child, just the child. That he won't press charges. That he wishes to be left in peace. He takes a shower; smokes, wrapped in his towel, out on the hotel balcony. Something is giving way in the sky; the sun is slowly slipping. He gets dressed; the room is still bright, just a hint of shadow in the corners, and through the open window the day casts a square of colour on the wall. The window frame quivers. The breeze swoops down on the afternoon, with reds, browns, ochres; the sea stretches out. He shaves, splashes on some lavender water. The open sea surges into the room through the three panels of the mirror. He behaves like someone getting ready to go out. He's developing habits. He has no appointments. He's going to have a drink on the casino terrace. The room grows even larger as the sun draws closer, its rays entering head on, unfolding walls and ceiling; the sea encroaches on the town and the sky. He hears children shouting on the beach, a school trip, recent arrivals, they're splashing around within a line of floating buoys; rounded up as the ropes are pulled in, they shriek with vexation as they're caught in the net. In the distance, over the steady rhythm of the waves, between the blue mirror and the open window throwing its glare on the wallpaper, the cries whirl like a flight of slow birds. The walls drift lightly; the wind is warm, supple, and the curtains flutter. The lighthouse has lit its lamp, barely brighter than the sky, the beam gliding over the untouched shadows. When he closes the door of his room, the lighthouse follows him down the corridors. The sky has taken on a mauve tinge, and a threadbare moon, quite pale, seems to be at the bottom of a stained-glass window. He could walk down like this every evening, having changed, along the cliff, to see how the tamarisks are doing, check on the guard-rail, say hello to Lopez, take a seat on one of the seafront terraces: the one at the cake shop, the one at the casino, the one where the orchestra plays during the tourist season.

He'd join the Cormorant Club, and all year round, in every kind of weather, he would take a dip in the ocean. Ordering his beer in front of the violet sea squeezed and rumpled by the evening, he wonders what makes a memory. This moment, in the rush of others, when he touches his lips to the froth, when the sea gives the silken rustle he thinks of as the sound of endless change, when the wind gently stirs hair and lifts up skirts – will he remember it? Will he remember this very same sky, this sun, this horizon? This lighthouse and this moon, stubbornly present at the meeting? The craters, with discernible outlines, and the Sea of Tranquillity, the Sea of Fertility, where the striped boot-prints of the astronauts must still be visible? When he relaxes, he sees, as if by surprise, people, and especially places – such and such a precise instant in this or that garden – without having had any indication at the time that that moment would become a memory, and with-out successive interpretations changing the image it leaves behind, gradually clearing away superimposed accents, inflexions, expressions, climates. He wonders what he will see, when he remembers the sea; and whether one can remember it as one does a garden or a face, keeping a single motionless, fixed moment of it, a moment never seen, never experienced, but that isn't an abstract of the rest; a moment of real time, empty but familiar, that solidifies as if in a mould, contracting into an object, a vignette, a fetish. She has just sat down, at a table next to his; he recognizes her, he doesn't even need to turn his head. She's alone. The child must be playing over by the water, she looks up from her reading now and then. Her gaze stops between book and sea, her lips part slightly, she looks as if she is praying. She's wearing little earpieces. From time to time her fingers move in the folds of her dress, pushing buttons. Her hair is red in the sunset, her cheeks still full of daylight. Her identity is so clear that a lump comes to his throat. He stands up, lets himself be carried away by the vast foolishness of the sea, by those waves, by that summer music. Smiling, he pulls out the chair in front of her.

For a second, she's sure she knows him, her heart races, her cheeks burn, she breaks off from her English lesson. But he merely asks if he can sit down, that's all, buy her a drink, she hardly hears him through the foam earpieces, she presses PLAY again. He doesn't push it, goes back to his own table, almost as if he was waiting; or he's just like everyone else, he's looking at the sea, watching the women, enjoying his holiday. The child will be back soon. She pays for her coffee, gets up, walks down to the edge of the water. Her heart gradually stops pounding.

She's never been so close before, it's quaking, shuddering beneath her feet. The water pulls away, spreads out, seems to increase: between the mass that has just collapsed, the froth that boils and seethes, there, close enough to touch her, and the surface rising behind it, sucking in and scooping out – it stretches, looking like the inside of a mollusc, steely blue, veined with white, an oyster, the underside of a tongue; it yawns without breaking, it's smooth, glossy, the lining of an organ they must pass through. They move closer still, Patrick's hand is crushing hers, they're standing in the surf and already the undertow is sucking them in, they have to plant their legs wide apart, bracing themselves. She looks at the other swimmers, the ones who hesitate stiffly on the edge, and those who are already on the other side; no one stays in the undertow, no one can survive in the undertow, in the void the waves exhaust themselves trying to fill, where the water somersaults, swells, then disappears, where air cracks, sand explodes, where nothing subsides or fills up. Patrick has dashed in still holding on to her; her arm is dislocated, her body crashes into the water (lemmings are small arctic rodents that leap in large numbers from the tops of ice floes), he told her not to breathe, to hold her breath tightly, even babies do that naturally (but they've retained their opercula like sea lions have), all around her it's white, snowy, she's the tiny figure shaken up in a snow-globe (don't breathe, let the heart beat), one day she'll try oxygen tanks and her lungs, by themselves, will unite water and earth. Suddenly everything grows brighter. The water is a big green eye glued to her eye, she sees into the depths of the watery pupil, through to the water's brain, the bubbles, the convolutions, the vortices, the uncertainties; then something tugs at her as if the sea wanted to call her back, resolve an ambiguity, a question, a doubt; Patrick holds on to her, she's clamped belly down to the sea bed, she's a flatfish and what she glimpses of her skin is sand-coloured, then everything lifts off (the astronauts in their shuttle experienced nothing more violent than this), the sea swirls above her, rips the water, something falls away far behind, she is the extreme tip of this batting eyelash, and the hard, crushed, compact sand slides away beneath her: the eye opens.

The sky is enormous, much larger than the sea. The sky doesn't touch her, keeps its distance, and the shore seems already so remote that she realizes you can drown from so much solitude, since a mere glance at the land, over there, at the houses, the terraces and the ice-cream man, is enough to make you feel abandoned (astronauts are trained not to go insane when they see the Earth, round and blue, smaller than their porthole). Her feet are dangling beneath her body; the water is green, opaque. Around them a few severed heads are grimacing in the sun and the salt sea, catching their breath. Now past the breakers, they are high up, well beyond the hollow, safe on the shoulder of the swell. Other waves arrive, rounded waves, tall and true: deep-sea waves, driving the tide. A depression curves between them, already dragging the body down, but there's no risk of vanishing into the abyss any more, only of drowning. 'Swim under!' yells Patrick. Only rollers that have already broken can be crossed on the surface, the body breasting the surf straight on. Otherwise you must dive, find the weak spot in the wave and break free of its suction. One moment you're escaping the sea, rediscovering the laws of the land, the body, the muscles; for one second you think you're in control – then you're beneath the whirlpool. And until you recognize the equilibrium of the sky, the light-house, the brightly coloured row of beach huts, you are afraid for one dizzying instant that you have found the way to the bottom of the sea.

They've passed beyond all the breakers. Out where they are (resting on the ocean as on the brow of an elephant), the sea is now only an immense rocking; a long way off, heavy feet strike the ocean floor; muscles ripple beneath the surface, shoulders roll above slopes of flat hide. The beach is dwarfed, stubby and gleaming at the bottom of the sky; from here, it seems like a migration after some cataclysm: the people are naked and tiny, massed at the edge of the water, advancing, hesitating, rushing forward; the town is deserted. Distance is constantly shifting, she doesn't know where to look on the curve of the water. A few waves come in at an angle from the open sea, she cranes her neck, tries to take advantage of the elephant's rolling gait. The waves break in profile, you can see the arch where salamander-skinned surfers appear in black flashes, the tube of emptiness the waves roll along and carry away. But it's difficult to see the wave truly. Should you isolate one spot in the tumbling water, mark it, following a drop, a whiteness, a brighter streak (too swift for the eye, yet slow enough for its fall to be recorded) – and return to the top again, quickly, picking out another spot, over and over, wave after wave? Or try to grasp the wave as a whole, the spume that disintegrates, breaks up, scuds away in scattered threads, endlessly spreading its net over a tremendous catch: shifting, fluid, and long gone.

The ocean has become the sea, with eddies, a current that forms a swell near the coast. Warning signs become more and more violent, flesh thrashes in alarm, water spurts more quickly beneath the broad gills. The body rises and falls, the land makes its noise, breaks the water, growls, roars, lying in wait like a huge predator. Now, no matter how arched its tail fin, open water has become inaccessible. The alarm falls silent, all is quiet in the massive movement of the waves. Fatigue has taken the place of hunger. The hollow beneath its worn whale-bone seems gradually to have closed; the sea no longer flows through it, meeting an obstacle now, a stillness, deep in the belly. The muscles needn't move to escape that hunger any more, and the body lets itself be borne along like a buoy. In the deep, in the abyss, wait giant squid, great white corpses flushed, in sudden tremors, with lurid colour. Far above, a few blue glints snag on the scales of transparent fish. Then the seaweed becomes increasingly green. Fierce, yet soothing, a breeze sweeps the water away, a cliff looms up, the light spreads out, botanic, while blue headlands grow larger and stretch long glittering fingers towards the water. The plankton thickens, there's good grazing here, jaws wide open, swimming in the warmth and nourishment, among the tiny shrimp that suddenly seem more numerous than water droplets. The cliff marks a rock ledge; the sea is a porridge, cooking on the continental shelf. Its lateral line quivers slightly, sensing, off towards a sandy depression, the faint presence of humans, the heat of those naked seals. There are several of them, a small group in the warm water, playing with the waves near the shore. Motors cough, the water gives little surges; a colony has taken up residence here. Taking one last reading with its lateral line, it avoids the beach. The cliff is quite close now, reflecting sound waves straight back: a clay mass, primordial, weathered by water, scarred by grottoes, rivulets, faults, magnetic conglomerations, and metal fallen from the sky. Its back breaks the surface, the air is brutally dry, the wind bends its dorsal fin and drives the body towards the rolling surf. From this point on sonar can no longer distinguish between up and down, north and south. A boulder slices deep into its flesh. Its flanks strike the sand amid retreating waves; it suffocates slowly beneath the weight of its muscles while its gills collapse from their own volume.

The land is harsh, imperious, sunk beneath its belly; the ground slews about under a motionless sun.

She twists her head round while four nurses are holding her down. She's been given an injection, tended to, tucked in, seen by a specialist. There's something below the cliff, in the triangular tag-end of the tidal wash, a strange boat at the water's edge, a yacht, perhaps. Its canvas appears to be black, as if the aged Aegeus were going to throw himself once again from the top of a cliff, and this time send the Atlantic into mourning. Because of the windows – firmly closed – and the reflections on the sea, it's hard for her eyes to establish the perspective. The sail hangs, thick, dark, and limp. She'd simply like to take one last look, admire the view, study this coast, enjoy the landscape a little longer. But they say that will only wear her out even more. The tourist season is beginning, she's probably a poor advertisement for the spa. They've telephoned her son-in-law; an ambulance is coming to collect her.

The basking shark (genus *Cetorhinidae*) can grow to the size of a small sperm whale. It is characterized by very large gills, a collar of red grooves so deep the head seems ready to separate from the body. A harmless living fossil, toothless, filtering krill like the baleen whales, it can attain a great age, witnessed by the concentric circles inscribed in its flesh (this can be prepared in slices, like tuna *à la basquaise*, but is little prized). It travels around the globe, solitary and open-mouthed, and a recent study by the Museum of the Sea has established that it voyages not at the mercy of the currents, as its apparent passivity and weak neuronal development might suggest, but following deliberate routes. Almost blind (like most sharks) and endowed with sensory equipment that is in fact quite sophisticated, its misleadingly monstrous and languid appearance has given rise to numerous legends (mermaids, sea serpents, gigantic submarines).

It's hard to know what she's looking at, what spot out at sea or in the empty air. Apparently she couldn't care less about that thing busy dying at the feet of all those onlookers. The local press is taking pictures; her kid has joined the schoolchildren on their holiday. He's been following her since yesterday and isn't nervous at all about leaving her; he'll find her again, the town or the beach always gives her back. She seems to follow the same routine every day: the big block of flats, the cake shop, the deckchair on the beach, the casino terrace. In order to listen to the official from the Museum of the Sea, the reporters, the teacher, and the schoolchildren have abandoned the bucket chain they'd formed for the shark. Big brown patches like parchment are slowly spreading, the moisture's evaporating, soon it will dry into dust like the jellyfish that leave behind, at low tide, only a crown of black salts around a sandy well. In the meantime, the sound it's making is so distressing that he can't really see himself swinging into action with this particular soundtrack, he would have preferred the waves alone, a bit of a breeze, the faraway rhythms of seaside music. The dreadful thing gasps and whimpers, you'd think it had lungs, its mouth grilled with whale-bone is open as wide as it will go, its tongue is black and swollen, it struggles for air. A moan is heard, something childlike, human, dogs sometimes have inflexions like that, it's difficult to believe that such a sound is coming from a creature whose body is so fantastically different from ours: it isn't an appeal, it isn't a rattle, it's a sob, the creature is sobbing. Luckily more and more seagulls are arriving, wheeling overhead in their hundreds, a brassy tempest of foam in the bend of the cliff; the official from the Museum of the Sea strains to make herself heard. She shrank back when she saw the cameras arrive. He goes closer. Had he still been looking for her, having trouble finding her, the town would have produced her for him here, it's a family photograph, everyone is gathered around the sideshow attraction: the little girl obviously – he's going to have to make up his mind – as well as the tourists, the reporters, the schoolchildren, the teacher, the educational staff from the museum, a lighthouse keeper, a swimming pool attendant, bellboys from the Grand Hotel, nurses and chambermaids from the thalassotherapy centre, gardeners, bistro owners, the seafront orchestra (who have only just woken up) together with some hostesses and a croupier from the casino, plus some jeering fishermen, people from the pleasure boats, the lifeguards, and that movie-star surfer who takes care of the kid, and that idiot of an estate agent who's hoping for a chance to see the mother, and the police, who are on the alert and have set up barriers to keep the onlookers away from the crumbling cliff, and the zoologists from the Museum (who will salvage the body with a winch, giving it the *coup de grâce* if need be; they're planning to have it stuffed), and even Lopez, who has moved his van to the top of the cliff, by the only path that leads to the steps. He's right beside her now. Her ability not to see him is so great, so stubborn, that it seems to be the result of a decision: after the previous day's episode she has completely ignored his presence, wearing her earpieces as she drinks her coffee, lying in her deckchair with her eyes closed behind dark glasses, gazing elsewhere out on the beach. Without looking her way, he speaks to her; she says nothing. The surfer has seen what he's up to, he's careful not to get involved. The kid has come closer, pretending to be still interested in the big fish, still part of the group of schoolchildren on their holiday. He gets out his mobile, and now the kid is really interested.

Here they are, all three of them, coming back up. He wonders if it's the father, makes a show of stacking some cones. The little girl is frighteningly pale, he fixes her a double cornet, chocolate-coated strawberry, he insists, on the house. It's the guy who thanks him, hands the ice-cream to the child. Something inside her is letting go, relaxing, he knows the ice-cream hasn't anything to do with it, but still, he feels good. During the month she's been here, he's watched her turn brown, maybe grow a bit – at that age they shoot up quickly – and even learn to swim, but in a kind of astonishment, a trance from which she's beginning to emerge; perhaps she's going to cry, or laugh. If that really is the father, then he went away and came back, his wife was waiting for him, they'd agreed to meet again on the coast.

Except that at least one of the suitors has got lucky, the whole town knows it, and this particular Penelope wasn't waiting for a man, or for anyone, to come back.

She has accepted a cornet as well, and that's a first. He's curious to see which flavour she'll pick; she chooses a sorbet of course, melon, she's the type who thinks a little leaf of lettuce is a meal. The guy declines the offer with a serious, almost professional air. He's working for somebody, that guy. Maybe it's something to do with spies, or blackmail, a criminal settling of scores. The coast, its reputation, its casinos, the border, they attract all sorts of people. The little girl is perhaps only a cover, a blind, a straw child. She's a sight, the mother, sucking away at her melon ice. Her face is the same today as it was a month ago. It makes you wonder if she noticed the days going by, the weather warming, the tides rising, summer arriving, the child growing up. In one month the sky has become deep blue, the leaves on the plane trees have turned their full green, the wind has widened its embrace. The mountains have receded, blurred by the heat, palest mauve over Spain. And the sea has built up to its summer strength, derived not from storms, but from constancy, the persistence of a broad and steady swell, voracious, thrusting mountains and horizon aside. The sea had to excavate as well, scouring the depths and the rock shelf, pounding full pelt on the coast, which creaks in the summer with a hot, metallic grinding. It's the moment, the longest day of the year, when regrets are tossed into bonfires, when dancers leap over the glowing embers and then gather up, in remembrance, a few cinders gone cold. The air is puffy, mild, powdery. She has that kind of skin, almost misty, as though it were loosely woven; it's as if only her dress were holding her here, in the mesh of its crossed shoulder straps, putting a barrier between the light and her body, which otherwise would vaporize, translucent and ethereal, in a sky full of pollen and spindrift. The sun is high in the heavens, where it waits, white and unwavering. It immobilizes the leaves of trees, the ruffled edges of waves, so curtailing gestures, so hemming in shadows, that you'd think the town were spellbound, and that this man, this woman, this child were transfixed in a solar stupor, waiting to revive, or else completely oblivious. A limousine, curtains drawn, is leaving the thalassotherapy centre; the limo floats, violently white, throwing light back on the funeral pyre of a town, beneath a sky ticking like the time mechanism of a bomb; the buildings, the sea – something is cracking, straining. Seagulls take off from the cliff, cyclists breeze by, a few waves break. He opens his mouth: the beautiful people are arriving, the biggest international stars come here to pursue their love affairs. He feels as though he were talking to shop-window mannequins. The guy has taken the little girl's hand. Off they go, the two of them. There was a kiss, a handshake, the woman is still here; her sorbet drips on to the ground in pink splodges, and occasionally on to the full, dark skirt which the wind, with an effort, is lifting up just a little. The ceremony is over, the cliff did not collapse. He wonders if he should call the police. She comes to life now, says goodbye to him, and walks off, throwing her cornet into a wastebin fixed to a tamarisk tree.

The city seems like a tracery of landing strips, hundreds of straight, twinkling, crisscrossing strips, a luminous game of spillikins. The flight attendant has announced their descent; baggage checked through to its final destination goes directly to the next airport on a night flight. She has a two-hour stopover, she'll ask the taxi to take the ring road. She now speaks simple and adequate English; she reserved her seat in English at the travel agent's and spoke English to the flight attendant. She's in training. When she doesn't have to show her passport, people take her for a foreigner; neither English – because of the accent – nor from here, obviously. In

Sydney, she'll find herself a little job, then she'll travel: the desert, the pillars of red rock, the virgin forest, the blue lagoons, ranches so vast you need several weeks to tour them on horseback, where riders use mirages, taking into account the heat and the time of day, to judge the distance to the next water hole. The incidence of skin cancer among the white population is the highest in the world; gaps are opening in the ozone layer. Washbasins drain clockwise because of the Coriolis force. The bush is infested with dingoes, the sea with man-eating sharks, a big canyon crosses Tasmania, land of waterfalls. There are daily flights to Hobart. A tunnel dug through the centre of the Earth would come out there, at the Antipodes. The plane is landing, she has to put away her guidebook. In the taxi she affects an English accent to give the name of the other airport, for long-distance flights. Her former address is ten minutes away, she's almost surprised to find it intact in her memory. At this hour the child must be asleep. The flat is dark, illuminated by the gleam of the street lights; the child breathes softly and evenly, there, at the end of the hall; on the left, there's the other bedroom; opposite, the living room. She would walk silently around, idly stroking the mantelpiece, crushing a ficus leaf between two fingers, and could pretend, in front of the furniture with its plump shadows, that dust sheets had been thrown over everything. She buys magazines to stock up for the twenty-hour flight, and a tracksuit in the duty-free shop. Everything is closing. The airport is emptying, there are only two more departures tonight, hers and one for Buenos Aires. She could have tackled Spanish: the pampas, the gauchos. Travellers in saris have stretched out between the luggage trolleys, kohl smeared beneath their closed eyes. A man smokes, his head nodding over a newspaper with some Asian celebrity she doesn't recognize on its front page. Cleaners sweep around the sleepers; paper wrappers flutter. The silence expands, thickened by breathing, sometimes fissured and set jingling by electronic chimes: you expect an announcement, a name launched by a voice saturated with air, a destination, a lost traveller, but you hear only a hissing, an error, a clumsy movement on the part of flight attendants slipping on their jackets. The airport fills with rustlings, papers being put away, the clink of glasses being stacked, a step, the slamming of a door, sometimes a laugh, faint chatter among invisible people: the fragmented atmosphere of a place one is leaving, amplified and made more distant than a world beyond the seas by the indifference of empty loudspeakers.

She gets a coffee from the vending machine, drinks it leaning against a bay window. The runways are deserted and quite brightly lit. A plane taxis slowly by. She plays at squeezing the light between her eyelashes into blurry stars. A group of old-age pensioners walks past, chatting in English; she finishes her coffee, straightens up to follow them. Boarding has begun.